D0879758

PRAISE FOR
THE HOROLOGIST

"An excursion packed with imagery, learning, and risk. Above all, McCarthy's book reminds us that life never stops teaching. The superb storytelling will captivate seasoned and budding readers alike."

—**LISA MAHER**, *contributor to* The Austin American Statesman

"Highly entertaining! You'll love this immersive novel, it's a riveting read!"

—**BRILLIANT LIU**, *creator of @House.of.Leaders (800k+ followers on Instagram)*

"McCarthy is a promising young writer with a proverbial old soul as he takes readers on a thought-provoking journey like that of a wise sage. It's a tantalizing must-read for all ages."

—**KIMBERLY KEY**, *expert at* Psychology Today *and author of* Ten Keys to Staying Empowered in a Power Struggle

"Ancient wisdom from a young voice . . . this story is destined for the 'classics' list!"

—**MARY BROOKE CASAD**, *author of* Bluebonnet of the Texas Hill Country, *and other children's books; co-author of* The Basics *bible studies*

"Take the time to read this thought-provoking novel. It's a page turner. You just might learn something along the way."

—REBECCA REYES, *author of* Fajita Fiesta *and other works in the cooking space.*

"*The Horologist* explores the deeper side of what it means to be human. That the story comes from such a young author is surprising, since its wisdom is usually the province of a person who has been long on this planet. While my own writing is more adventure and story-centered, I can appreciate a more meaningful tale—*The Horologist* appears to offer just such an adventure!"

—JESS THORNTON, *author of* Mailman Tales, Driftless Mailman, *and many other novels*

"*The Horologist* is a MUST READ for everyone who wants to maximize the fulfillment of their life . . . an entertaining journey of personal discovery where characters find adventure, love and eternal gems of wisdom. The attention to detail and vivid descriptions compel the reader forward to see where the story leads. It inspires people to consider their current actions and how they will influence their future."

—RICHARD V. BATTLE, *author of* The Four Letter Word That Builds Character

"An uplifting, engaging read. This story fosters a reader's introspection, causing an appreciation of what life and happiness are all about."

—RICK ZEHRER, *Brigadier General, United States Air Force*

"*The Horologist* deploys witty and attention-grabbing storytelling that will captivate your attention. An exciting read from cover to cover, this tale is a must read for young and old alike. McCarthy manages to impart pragmatic and impactful life lessons while keeping the reader captivated by his vivid and colorful descriptions and cast of memorable characters."

—FELIX AKOMPI, *Founder of Energie Row and previous senior management at Royal Dutch Shell*

"A rebellious and refreshing escape form daily life to embark on an adventure of self-discovery. Clearly just the beginning of an exceptional career as an author."

—DR. DAWN BUCKINGHAM, *Texas Senator for District 24*

The Horologist

by Miles McCarthy

© Copyright 2018 Miles McCarthy

ISBN 978-1-63393-598-3

All rights reserved. No part of this publication may be reproduced, stored in a retrieval system, or transmitted in any form or by any means—electronic, mechanical, photocopy, recording, or any other—except for brief quotations in printed reviews, without the prior written permission of the author.

This is a work of fiction All the characters in this book are fictitious, and any resemblance to actual persons, living or dead, is purely coincidental. The names, incidents, dialogue, and opinions expressed are products of the author's imagination and are not to be construed as real.

Published by

köehlerbooks™

210 60th Street
Virginia Beach, VA 23451
800-435-4811
www.koehlerbooks.com

THE
HOROLOGIST

MILES MCCARTHY

VIRGINIA BEACH
CAPE CHARLES

PROLOGUE

"OLIVER, YOU ACT like you have it all figured out. Take a moment, step back, and examine the convictions so deeply ingrained in your life. Do this, and you will find that you have tethered yourself in commonality and wrapped yourself in false chains. You know it as well as I: You are much more than you pretend to be."

The voice paused. Its source, ambiguous and obscure.

"For some time, I have wondered how you can be so awake, yet so unaware of your potential. So, here we are . . . and in more ways than one, it is the examination of your destiny which brings us together."

With those words, the voice was gone.

Oliver shook to. He found himself sitting at a nouvelle table, looking extravagant but not feeling it. He wore a seven-fold tie and beneath that a virile suit. The restaurant he sat in, the Bel Étage, was a cold tundra of stylish bravado and contemporary décor. The tables were scattered about like little islands of privacy and the misty climate in whole was chilling.

At his table, Oliver's breath condensed and atomized over his plate as he scanned the room. To his left, a heavy snow poured over a skyline of pencil towers and soaring constructs. To his right, inside the Bel Étage, suits and silk dresses occupied the bar, waiting to be seated; and at the front of the room, a grand piano sat beneath a staircase rising to an unmarked door.

Oliver looked down at his own table. On the cloth with the silverware was an arrangement of sapphire roses and a bottle of white wine. He then moved his eyes across the table, and though he sensed a presence, he couldn't make out who the figure was. A strange fog clouded his view. Oliver stared, sharpening his eyes, but he couldn't pierce the mist.

Oliver nervously arranged the napkin in his lap and picked up his flatware as he prepared to eat. But before he could, an elderly gentleman appeared at his side. "Mind if I join you?"

Oliver paused, nodded approval, then tasted his first bite.

The man pulled up a chair and let out a relaxed breath. "Things are a bit odd tonight, don't you think?"

Oliver swallowed and glanced up to inspect his guest. The man had the type of face that would age little over the years, but he looked like a typical buff—until Oliver locked onto his eyes. If they hadn't been seated so close, he would have missed them. Those eyes. On the surface, of usual fashion. But he could somehow see behind them, like a filmy conception was tunneling from within.

Oliver, growing more guarded, spoke. "Quiet indeed. I'm—"

His guest interrupted. "I'm well aware of who you are, Oliver. That was decided a long time ago. The question now is who you might be."

Oliver looked across the table again. He still could see nothing behind the cloud. His guest continued, "You are capable of becoming someone great, Oliver. Remember that, because interesting things are afoot, my friend." The man gestured over Oliver's shoulder. "The storm; it seems to be fading."

Oliver shifted to look outside. The snowfall was gone and the skyline appeared to be warming.

When Oliver turned back to continue the discussion, his guest had receded into the blur. And next to Oliver's fingers lay a note and a silver pocket watch. He straightened the parchment and absorbed these words slowly and methodically:

> *Once, I dreamt myself a butterfly fluttering hither and thither. I was conscious only of my happiness as a butterfly, unaware of any manhood.*
>
> *Then I awoke, and I was veritably myself. But, now, I do not know whether I was then a man, dreaming myself a butterfly, or whether I am now a butterfly, dreaming myself a man.*

Oliver reread the note, then lifted the clock. It was heavy, palm-sized, and cast in a fiery charcoal finish. He held it surprisingly tight, gripping it as if he were waiting for it to pulse. Oliver looked closer, and at the top of the trinket, above the Roman numeral *XII*, was an engraving of two butterflies.

Oliver sighed and took the parchment, creased it over the pocket watch, and placed the gift in the lining of his jacket.

Then he finished his meal.

THE WATERCOLORIST

OLIVE SKIN LINED his frame. Russet hair crowned his head. The boy was as charming as he was tall, as brave as he was humble . . . but what defined Oliver was his aloofness. He never let anyone know exactly who he was, and because of this, everyone only knew a side of him. He was a Rubik's Cube, unsolved; a chameleon camouflaging his innermost desires.

Oliver grew up with his mother and father in a Spanish town near Cantabria. His father was an engineer, and his mother was in photography. The three of them lived comfortably and simply, and had more than enough—and they were happy because of it.

Oliver was popular and well liked, but everyone said that his mind was always in another place, like he was looking for something that no one could offer. What people didn't understand was that Oliver had found what he was looking for; he had found something that captivated his heart and gave him purpose, and her name was Isabella.

Isabella lived in a neighboring town, and until Oliver accompanied his mother on a photography job one day, he had no idea how empty life had been.

On the car ride over, Oliver's mother handed him her backup camera. "I'll be at the wedding reception for a while. Why don't you take this and go get some shots?"

When they arrived, Oliver received a hug from his mother, looped the camera sling around his neck and started walking. At first, he was unsure of what to capture, but as he settled in, he began to see the charm of this new landscape. The town was picturesque, with old baroque architecture and softer stucco buildings. Oliver snapped stills of bicycles resting against walls and of residents walking along the streets. He paused to examine his collection when he first heard her voice.

"Let's see what you've got."

Oliver looked up to find a tanned girl his age reaching for the camera. She smiled as she guided the screen towards her, forcing Oliver to move closer as the sling pulled against his neck. He studied her impassive green eyes and brunette hair as she flipped through the album. "You're missing something. Come with me."

Isabella set the camera against Oliver's chest and led him around the corner. The street opened into a roundabout, and on the adjacent side was an impressive cathedral with florid ornamentation and a maze of pediments.

The girl's voice was spirited. "There's your shot."

And for the rest of the afternoon, Oliver and Isabella perused the streets. There was a connection there, an encouraging energy that resonated between them. Isabella was decisive and energetic and saw a challenge in bringing a reserved, methodical boy out of his shell.

When Oliver was back in front of the reception, Isabella gave him her number, and for the remainder of that summer, each time his mother was called in, Oliver would go along to see Isabella. Weeks passed and the closer they became, the more they both felt like nothing was missing from life. Eventually, they began taking bikes into the countryside, where their imaginations infused, and their hearts aligned. The universe seemed to center in on them. Time seemed to stop.

But one day, Isabella told Oliver that her parents were getting divorced, and that she was moving to Barcelona with her mother. Isabella gave Oliver her new number, but when he tried to call, the line was out of service. He tried twice more with the same result, and from then on, the boy and girl lost touch.

When Isabella left, everything changed for Oliver. A feeling of emptiness emerged, and a large void quietly grew. Life without Isabella, without the warmth of love, just didn't make sense.

It was a brilliant summer day. Oliver and Leo were strolling through the town when an idea emerged.

Oliver looked at his closest friend, who had dirty-blonde locks, broad shoulders and round chest. "Leo, has life has grown predictable? Sometimes I feel like I've become too set in my ways."

"And what do you propose we do about it?"

"Let's go somewhere we've never been. Do something we haven't done." Oliver scanned the stone street around him. His eyes stopped on a narrow alley tucked between two buildings. Deep within the shadow, something sapphire fluttered in the dark. Oliver edged forward and looked into the alley. The sight came again.

Without a word, Oliver raced down the passage. Leo followed, hollering to his friend and staying on his heels as they made their way through the gloom.

When the boys emerged on the other side of the alley, they were flooded with sunshine. Oliver swiveled his head in the light, searching for what he thought he saw.

Leo was panting, his hands on his knees. "Oliver, are you mad? Next time let's agree on the unpredictability."

As Leo caught his breath, he stood. "Where are we?"

The boys were in a small courtyard. A light breeze stirred, and seated under the shade of a wide tree, a man known as Winslow was finishing up his latest watercolor piece. He sat perched on his stool in a sapphire sweater, taking the tip of his brush brush from his palette up to the canvas.

Clamped to the easel was a portrait of a woman in remarkable detail. But what caught the boys' attention were her features; they were disassembled across the frame. Her jaw was not below her cheeks. Her nose wasn't beneath her brow. Winslow had spread her beauty across the canvas, and yet, there was something so real about her too. Something that transcended his brush.

The boys watched from a distance as he painted her lips. When Winslow paused, they walked up behind him.

"Who is that you're painting?" Oliver asked.

Winslow turned over his shoulder and found two timid boys observing him. He was kind when he spoke. "Oh, just someone who wishes to be painted."

"How did you learn to paint like that?" Leo asked.

"Like everyone else. Don't you know how?"

Leo shook his head.

"It just takes practice. Have you ever tried?"

Another head shake.

"Well. There's the problem."

Oliver nodded towards the easel. "But who is she?"

"Someone I once knew." He paused but could see that Oliver was looking for a real answer. "This woman helped guide me on my journey. You see, boys, I am a traveler by choice and a painter by profession, but above all, I'm a self-actualizing man."

Leo looked from the woman on the easel to Winslow. "What's self-actualization?"

Winslow painted while he answered. "It's a lot like art. Each is an endless process by which you constantly seek the causes of your own ignorance. Do either of you know what makes a piece of art or a person great?"

The boys shrugged.

"Great art and great people teach us. They make their audiences aware of an overlooked or underappreciated part of their lives."

Winslow touched his brush to the red paint, swirled it with the yellow, and then took the bristles up.

Leo spoke beside the stool, "But why did you paint her like that?"

Winslow smiled, but underneath, a jolt of sorrow flashed across his face as his eyes turned to black apertures.

"This woman was my wife, and she passed years ago. After she left, one morning on a long walk, I dozed off under a grove and I dreamt a powerful dream. In this dream I found myself at a crossroad. I looked to my left and saw my old life—a life full of consumption and momentary pleasures. I saw a false sense of security. In this dream, I then turned to my right and what I saw frightened me. I found myself looking into an abyss; it was a void I had felt my whole life but not seen until then. I turned back and re-examined my old life, but I suddenly felt hollow, and it was in that moment that I knew I had to leave it behind.

"I faced the void and stepped forward, blind and uncomfortable and utterly vulnerable, but I kept moving. I shivered in the unknown and ached in the obscure, but the farther I walked the more I found myself growing stronger. For some time, I was alone in the dark, but my spirit lifted when I came to a path which led me out of this tunnel, a path which led to a life I never knew. As I continued on, the ether around me began to grow lighter, and eventually I was led to my wife. I knew I was dreaming, but somehow, I understood that she was really there, clear as day, painting a picture on a stool—of me.

"Suddenly, I awoke back in the grove under a fresh sun. I felt enriched and anew, and I have been on this path ever since. So, I paint her as I do because as much as I am alive and well and fulfilling my vision, without her next to me, I can never be whole."

The boys stepped forward and studied the woman in greater detail. There was a remarkable sense of emotion in the air.

Oliver looked up, "Winslow, how do we find paths of our own?"

"I don't know which path you should take, but I can help show you the way. Begin by asking yourself what you love to do. What is that one thing that you could wake up every day and do happily for the rest of your life? It's okay to not know what it is right now, but if you haven't found it yet, keep looking, and don't settle along the way."

He turned to the woman's portrait. "Go out into the world and find what you love, then do everything you can to hold onto it. Do that, and you'll be free."

Leo looked down at his feet like a timid boy. "But I'm so young! How am I supposed to know what I want to do? What if I can't find my path?"

Winslow set down his tools and fully turned from the canvas. His tone was firm and absolute. "Never, ever, think like that. It doesn't matter how old you are, where you're from, or how much you have; you are here to fulfill a purpose." Winslow grinned. "In fact, your youth is an advantage. You have so much ahead of you. Time is on your side now more than it ever will be."

Oliver and Leo perked up.

"When you're young you have more time to take risks, to find out who you are, to fail. In that process, you will realize just how little you actually need and how much you can truly accomplish. You will see that nothing can stop you. And as you push beyond your boundaries and break through adversity, you will only grow stronger."

The boys took to Winslow. The world seemed a bit brighter and their spirits lifted a little higher with these words. Oliver looked at the other pieces of artwork Winslow had under the shade.

"How did you find time to paint all these?" Oliver asked. "It must've taken you forever."

Winslow chuckled. He began to paint the view of a man who had fulfilled his purpose. "Once my path was in sight, I knew I couldn't rest until I saw it through. As I began to paint, I realized how little time we have, and how fulfilling a dream really comes down to how you use it. Think about it. Everyone only has twenty-four hours a day. Everyone. The billionaire and the beggar. So, the quality of your life is dependent upon how you use those hours. Remember that. And understand that fulfilling a dream is not as complex as it seems; you just have to give something back to the world, and the very first thing you must give back is time."

Winslow put his finishing touches on the easel. He looked to the boys for reassurance. "What do you think?"

The boys nodded in amazement.

"Off you go, boys. Think on what I've said."

Oliver and Leo exited through the main gate of the courtyard and continued along, and as they ambled, Oliver found himself lost in thought. Winslow had made an impression. The truth had stung at first, but he realized with cutting honesty that most of his time had been spent pointlessly.

With each step, Oliver began to escape the machinery of his mind, as he considered: *Life is so backwards. The more that you steer away from the usual path, the more interest you draw and the more unique you become.*

This idea trickled into the boy, and like a compass needle aligning north, the inclination of his heart began to shift. Veil after veil peeled back as Oliver realized everything he hadn't done. Where he was, who he was, and what he was, was not enough. It was clear that the comfort from his mother and father, and the familiarity of his village, would not always make him happy. At last, Oliver decided: He would find his own path in life, and to do so, he needed to leave behind the safety and comfort he once knew.

As they made their way home, Oliver expressed this insatiability to Leo. He explained that he wanted to leave town for the summer, and how he wanted Leo to join, and that both their lives would be richer and fuller and more exciting because of it.

The two discussed the feasibility, and as virtuous thinkers do, they debated the idea and analyzed the outcomes.

"Where would we go?"

"I've always wanted to see Moscow."

"Too cold. Paris?"

"Too compact."

And this continued.

"How do we travel?" And again, the conversation took them into every nook and cranny. Then Oliver came to a realization. "Where we go and how we get there isn't the question. The question is why."

Oliver impatiently tended to the meal his mother prepared. He roosted at the table with a leg out the door, stabbing at the food like it was his first time using a knife and fork. When a break in conversation came, Oliver addressed his parents. "Mother. Father. I want adventure in my life. I want to get out and see the world. You have always supported me . . . I'd like permission to travel for the summer."

The boy raised his hand. "Before you say anything, know that I have thought this through. I understand that uncertainty lies at the edge of our town, but it is this uncertainty where I must go." He carried on for a while and revealed that Leo would be joining him on the journey.

Oliver's mother could see great determination in her son. "The desire to grow is natural and ordinary, Oliver; it is almost a universal sense of responsibility within us. I must ask, though, what do you expect to receive from such a journey?"

Oliver responded quickly. "To find my way, Mother; to start to become someone. I may stay here and age comfortably, but I sense that I will never be fulfilled. Or I may go out into the unknown and age uncomfortably, but find fulfillment."

His parents understood their son's thirst. They each had once known such a drought in their hearts. And, years ago, they fulfilled each other with love. It was time for their son to find his own fulfillment.

His father took a draw of tea. "And what will you do, Oliver? When you become someone?"

Oliver leaned on the quiet for a moment. "Just what you have done. Provide for my family, and give back to people around me and those in need."

These words settled his father. "This desire you have—fulfillment. It's an arduous path. But this path will make you stronger and wiser for enduring its difficulty. Oliver, this may sound harsh, but if you go, I want you to leave for much longer. Your mother and I will always be here, and so will the safe path. So, go out until you find what you're looking for, and don't come back until you do. My son, you are destined to become a man that the world needs. Break out of your shell, clear your mind, open your heart, and you will find the person you were meant to become. Take the night to think this through."

Oliver's decision did not change after the moon had come and gone.

The next morning, before he departed, Oliver was presented with an envelope. He opened it, smiled at his parents, and happily stored the money in his pack. The boy kissed his mother, embraced his father, gave one last nod, then left the village with Leo.

And just like that, they were on their way.

THE TROUPER

WITH PALMS WRAPPED around their packs, Oliver and Leo marched along the road leading from home. Beads of sweat flowed from their brows as they reached the town's outskirts. The boys had been this far before, but this time it was a deeper goodbye.

To the right of the crossroad was a cairn, and it spoke to them in the moment. The marker symbolized the stability they came from and the sturdy homes they could one day return to. But it was time for the boys to build their own foundations.

Facing the crossroad, Oliver asked Leo, "Which way should we go?"

They stood and watched as different people took different routes to different lives. Then a whistle blew.

It came from the bed of a cargo truck. Inside was a friendly fellow with a dirty shit and an open collar. He waved them in, and as the truck peeled off, Oliver and Leo looked back towards home with pride. They were rolling along with life.

"Name's Frakkoh, but people call me Freddie."

The passenger shook their hands. Freddie was a convivial character of high-voltage. His hair was stiff and golden-brown, and he wore a scraggly beard of four days. Freddie was a solo musician out on the road. He'd been at it for months, and when he spoke of his love for music, he did so with a daring level of effeminate mannerisms.

"People don't believe me, but I've always known I was born to play music. I used to rush home from school to learn a new song, then wake up before class to do the same. I just had to keep at it for a long time before I got any good.

"Then one morning, I was sitting on my porch with a guitar in my lap and a notebook in hand. I was looking out to the ocean tide, trying to come up with lyrics, but something deeper was speaking to me."

Freddie's voice was smooth, but intense.

"I watched set after set of waves ripple up and crash into the surf. Suddenly, my hand started writing. I looked down and the words were coming with ease. I rushed to the studio and recorded the song, and it became my first hit. I've been out here traveling ever since. So, that's how I got right here. I've just been riding my break."

Freddie pressed out a yawn. "People say I'm crazy for following my dream. They say I'm taking too much risk. But honestly, I think they're the crazy ones. A life without a dream is insane, to me."

Freddie pulled a booklet from his jeans, unwound the marbled cover, then tossed it across the bed.

Oliver and Leo held the journal between them. Many pages were folded, some torn, and it came with a heavy odor of smoke and fried food. Inside was like a mad scientist's notes. As the boys lined through, it was clear that the moxie of his songwriting birthed a unique style.

Leo looked up. "Freddie, how do you get up on stage and sing and perform? I'd—"

Freddie knew what he was about to say. "My friend. Fear is a compass; it tells you what you have to do to grow. Afraid of being by yourself? Become a lone wolf. Scared of asking a girl out? Walk up and get rejected. Fear the spotlight? Force yourself to bask in it. If you master fear, you can master yourself."

"But how did you get people to believe in you?"

Freddie laughed. "First, I had to believe in myself. But music has never been about the rewards or trophies, it's about the expression of who I am."

Freddie stretched out against the railing. "Look, life is hard, but a normal life is hell. I figure, if I'm going to take some punches anyway, I might as well take them doing what I want."

Oliver and Leo flipped through a few more of his pages. Bold black sharpie had crossed out lyrics. Oliver flipped the journal to Freddie. "No good?"

"Better believe it. Took months before something good finally came. But the wonderful thing is that you can become great at anything if you just put in the time. It's just that few are willing to stand against the headwind long enough to see their work blossom. Most people quit too early or never even start. You know how it is. You hear people saying they want to do this or that, but they don't do anything about it."

Freddie and the boys then exchanged stories for hours. The newcomers mainly listened except when Freddie asked what Oliver and Leo were doing there in the truck bed.

Oliver replied. "We're doing the same as you: just out looking for our break."

Freddie beamed. "I love it. A token of advice as you do—don't lend much credence to the opinions of others. If someone is encouraging and trustworthy, that's one thing. But negative opinions are only reflections of people's own fear."

The conversation pivoted to the boys' plan. When Freddie learned of their open-ended travel, he invited them to his next show. "Ever been to a *chiringuito?*"

The boys hadn't.

"It's like a beach bar. I think you'll love it."

Freddie leaned back against the truck bed. His guitar was to his right, his pack was to his left, and two new friends to his front. Freddie was happy the boys were tagging along. He didn't see Oliver and Leo as inexperienced boys on some flare of a summer trip. He saw them as brothers, as partners to share a journey with, however temporary or permanent their time together would be.

THE DREAM

NEAR SUNDOWN THE cargo truck turned on a road cut into the side of a hill—cliff above, sea below—and down towards the coast of Barcelona.

The driver threw the wheels onto the shoulder and braked stiffly. Freddie and the boys extended an arm over the side and leapt to the street. They reached back for their gear and nodded to the driver before the taillights reddened and the truck drove off.

When Freddie and the boys turned around, the *chiringuito* rrevealed itself. It sat on a beach plot sectioned off with railway posts and oversized rope. Inside was a stage, a white stucco bar and umbrellas, and a young crowd spread across the cool sand.

Oliver and Leo grinned as they looked around and questioned whether they were in paradise. The *chiringuito* was a sea of gorgeous people on a gorgeous coast.

Freddie was backstage for an hour before the stage simmered. The crowd gathered in front as the fanfare began a low roar, and with a stream of light, Freddie rushed forward as his voice exploded through the microphone. His vocals were as clear and loud as a trumpet, and when his voice brushed your ear, the heaviness of life receded. The crowd picked up their dancing and the probability of seduction soared with it.

Oliver was almost back from to the restroom when something caught his eye—the petals of a sapphire rose. There was something reminiscent in that color; something that made him stop and stare at the flower.

The petals sat over the ear of a dream. She was across the crowd, laughing and dancing amongst friends. Her impassive green eyes relaxed underneath her brunette hair. She wore a white half-slip that ended a few lengths above her knees, and her long, tanned legs glistened in the nightlight. The thought came like a lucid dream—*Isabella?*

Oliver was shaken, and in no coincidence Isabella rose up and looked over. She recognized the boy, but years had passed since they saw each other, and she couldn't figure out how she knew him. But Isabella parted her lips and smiled at the familiar face, and in that moment, Oliver's soul expanded.

"Oliver . . . Leo . . . get up here!"

Oliver's name came over the loudspeaker. Freddie had finished a song and was calling him and Leo onstage. Oliver froze, his heart racing. Leo rushed over and pulled him.

Onstage in the spotlight, Freddie introduced the boys to the crowd and spoke of their trip. The fans roared and cheered and agreed to treat them like royalty. Freddie then brushed them off with a wink and the boys descended back onto the beach.

As they stepped down, Oliver could feel a pair of eyes engulfing his every step. Isabella was staring at him. She and her friends had edged their way to the stage and were only a few paces away. On the sand, Oliver hesitated, but not for long. He purposely moved past her before he heard her voice.

"Oliver?"

His ears were ringing. She recognized him. He bucked the flow of the crowd and moved towards her. On the surface, he was relaxed, but inside, he rattled with the restlessness of a caged tiger.

"Is it really you?" She advanced towards him.

Neither Oliver nor Isabella could keep their eyes off the other. Isabella's voice turned defensive as she asked what they both were thinking. "What happened? Why did you never call?"

After Oliver explained himself, he asked her the same.

"I waited for your call, and it never came. I thought you didn't want to talk to me. It broke my heart." Then the moment shifted. Isabella gave Oliver a smile, turned, and headed deeper into the crowd.

His dial turned to ten. Their connection resurged. His heartbeat raced as he followed her into the mass.

They bounced in cadence as they maneuvered through the sea of bodies. In the wattage they danced, and Oliver took in a brilliant feeling, like when you know you're coming to a turning point in life.

As the show continued, Oliver was so immersed in the moment that he considered doing what he had been wanting to do for a long, long time—pour his eyes into hers and kiss her. So, he imagined what would happen if he did—what would pan out if he took this break.

Before he did, a fearful thought came: *What if she jerks back?* She might giggle at his sincerity, and pull away with a smile and a wagging finger. She would tease him, and Oliver would go crazy, because the tease harps on an instinctual desire: We always want what we can't have.

So, electively, Oliver let the moment pass. He danced and entangled himself with Isabella, and the heat of their bodies acclimated as the music pulsed and their hips locked. Their rhythms were the same, and each chord in the beat elevated and merged them.

Isabella reached her arm around the back of Oliver's neck, shifted towards him and soaked in his eyes. She once again found him addictive and appealing. She found him refreshing and genuine, and all her old feelings started to come backcome back . . . and this terrified her.

She released him and suddenly turned away and dotted her path out of the crowd.

Hypothermia swept through Oliver. His throat contracted. He raced after her, following Isabella's ebbing path. With every second, her route faded as the people bobbed and weaved with the music. Oliver pushed forward, half-guessing his way towards the edge of the crowd. On the fringe, he stopped. A glimmer came. Sapphire. A deep-blue rose Isabella was exiting the concert, alone. Oliver leapt and caught up with her outside the fence. "Isabella! What happened? Why are you leaving?"

There was trepidation in her eyes. She didn't say anything. But Oliver understood what signaled her alarm. He felt it too. It was a longing to be connected as strongly as possible. It was something he never thought he could feel. Something intoxicating.

There are things that you only get to do once in your life. There are moments that define who we are and capture the grand design of our souls. This is one of them—the first time you kiss the person you love.

Neither let go as a hypnotic pull brought them together. Their pulses were galloping, and in an adrenalized move, a catalyzed action, Oliver placed his lips against hers, and kissed her deeply.

When the cover lights came on and the concert ended, Isabella gave Oliver a coquettish smile, locked her fingers in his, and dragged him along to find her friends. He observed his fellow males, their faces full of jealousy as he marched along. He loved every step of it. How he devoured every stare.

When Isabella found her friends, everything had fallen into place. Leo was with one of them. Aisha was a languorous blond with cornflower blue eyes and fluttering lashes. She was in a pale orange sundress, which did her no harm, and she had the level of appeal that sprinkles into your mind long after you've left her side.

When the boys saw each other, they smiled, and Oliver nudged Leo, "Remember that girl I told you about?"

The foursome slid backstage to congratulate Freddie. He hugged the boys and introduced himself to the girls, then informed them all that the he had received a hotel suite in town, and invited the boys to stay.

The group ventured into the city that night, and ended up back in the suite listening to Freddie play the guitar. Everyone in the bunch clicked, and once again nothing was missing from life.

When they finally stopped and picked up their heads, it was nearly sunrise, so the girls decided to stay in the hotel. Freddie took the master, the girls took the guest room, and the boys took the sofas. But when Oliver's head hit the pillow, he couldn't help but notice the overpowering quiet around him. It was dead silent. No footsteps anywhere; not even the tiniest sound could be heard. Oliver had never known such quiet.

Something eerie was there, a cold energy coming from the other couch. Oliver turned over and looked at his friend.

A sliver of moonlight slanted in through a gap in the living room curtain. Leo was still, but Oliver could feel that he was awake. He could feel the capillary trickle of uncertainty and apprehension dripping into Leo's mind.

What is wrong?

THE MARES

IT WAS LONG past sunrise when Oliver awoke. The balcony door was open, and the ocean breeze tapped the thin blinds against the pane. Oliver looked across the room to find Leo's sofa vacant. The suite was quiet still, but now without that cold energy. Oliver tossed his blanket over the cushions and rose to inspect the suite.

Oliver tiptoed to the guest room and set his ear against the girls' door. He knocked quietly, then slid it open. Empty. Oliver then moved to the master. Empty. The suite was deserted.

Oliver had a biting sense of disappointment until he found a clue. Sitting on the kitchen table was a fresh breakfast and a message on a notepad. It read: *Beach*.

Oliver sat to eat just as a luminous butterfly floated in through the balcony door and hovered above the room. The butterfly had pink stripes stretching across its blue back. Oliver set down his fork and watched as the butterfly fluttered over him with a subtle affinity. He gaped with awe.

The butterfly was there no more than a blink when, like a kite in the wind, it lofted up and floated back outside.

Oliver stood and followed the manifestation out into the sun. But, by the time he made it to the balcony, all he found was the sight of morning commuters and the peaceful shoreline in the distance. The butterfly simply was not there.

Oliver stepped back in, cheated, but relieved. He could assign no meaning to the sequence that just played out. The butterfly singed the margins of Oliver's mind as the reverie turned back on itself. The sapphire phantom was unprovable, but the image of the butterfly lodged itself deep inside Oliver's subconscious.

Oliver sat in silence while he ate. When breakfast was over, he walked to the bathroom, plugged the sink, and doused his face with cold water. He stared into his glossy irises for a long time before he snapped back to.

Downstairs, summer hit Oliver with a fresh wave of heat. The white strip of sand outside their hotel was thinly occupied on this weekday morning, so finding his group of sunbathers was far from a challenge.

The girls! A billow of calmness came to Oliver as he remembered that he was on an adventure with his oldest friend, a new one, and two belles.

Had he brought a camera, this image—his friends resting on towels beneath a thirsty sun—would have made a fine postcard. Oliver resumed his hike towards them.

With his back to the water, Freddie lowered his sunglasses. "There he is!" The others turned and waved. Oliver took a seat on the foot of Isabella's chaise and let his head fall back and rest on her stomach. She didn't say anything, so he left it there with the whole day in sight.

There was a stretch of comfortable moments where everyone just sat, looked at the waves crashing in the surf, and took it all in.

Isabella then stood and made her way towards the tide. The surge reached her thighs, then it brushed her outstretched hands before she shut her mouth and dove in. Oliver watched her go, then snatched a towel and wandered down to shore.

Isabella glowed as she tromped out, water glittering off her physique as she plucked the towel from Oliver's hand and headed up.

By the time their frames had reddened, Freddie picked up what was going on. "So, girls. What next?"

Aisha looked at Isabella. "We're around Barcelona for two weeks then off to Majorca Isle at the end of the month."

Freddie knew what to say. He was the kind of guy you didn't have to explain things to. "Wonderful. I hear Majorca is perfect this time of year. Oliver, Leo, on our way in, didn't you two mention that you were planning on going there?"

The boys were taken aback by the forwardness, but also anxious to hear a response. They watched the girls, hoping they'd buy the story and that Freddie knew what he was doing.

Isabella rolled over on her towel and flipped her sunglasses up. She spoke to the group but was addressing Oliver. "You guys should tag along . . . you know, for safety." She seemed like she wanted to wink but at the last second held back.

Oliver cleared his throat while thinking of a response, but Freddie took the reins. "Isabella, great idea. Unfortunately, my schedule takes me north from here, but I wish you four the best."

"Oh, too bad, Freddie." Isabella paused for a moment as a thought ran through her head. She again looked at Oliver. "You know, my parents are in Italy for a while. We have a guest house you two could stay in."

Oliver glanced at Leo, looking for confirmation.

"Perfect, Isabella."

While the girls went up to the hotel, Oliver and Leo thanked Freddie for everything he had done. "Thanks for it all, Freddie. It was nice to have known you, however briefly."

He came back with a handshake for each. "Listen, boys, keep in touch, you hear?" But when you take a rolling stone like Freddie, the boys knew they never would. And that was that, and it was perfectly all right.

Oliver and Leo decided to get their own transportation, and rented a pair of Vespa scooters to snail through Barcelona during their stay.

When the foursome arrived, Isabella's house was not what Oliver expected. It sat above a dark-blue lake on a hill carpeted with orchards and green-ribbon fields.

The house itself was a jewel of architectonics. In fact, calling the estate a house was a disservice to its designer, who happened to be Isabella's stepfather—a renowned architect. Every piece of the structure, inside and out, was purposively crafted, including the garden of pink caper trees out back. However, something on the estate grounds flustered Oliver and kept him alert. There was a vague barrier reverberating across the property. Something defensive.

The boys stayed in the guest house for two weeks. They took things slow and called home periodically, and their parents were relieved that the boys were not so far away.

At month-end, the group loaded the Vespas onto a ferry and sailed to Majorca for the weekend. They swam in the clear water, toured the tropics, and enjoyed the festivities along the beach. The sugary-blue and chrome scooters were stopped on a street when Aisha took her arms off Leo. "Isabella, what about our summer tradition?"

Isabella smiled. Apparently, this was a good idea.

The rest of that day was driven by instinct. The two couples were riding horses along a rocky bluff when the girls peeped at each other. On cue, the brown mares parted ways, and the dates peeled off in opposite directions towards the water.

Oliver and Isabella found rhythm trudging through the sand as the sea air fleeced their faces. When they reached an inlet, Isabella dismounted and walked along the beach to take in the final bands of sun. Oliver pulled a blanket from the saddle and followed. They lengthened out in true pacification as the red rays began to slip over the horizon.

The fluidity of the whitecaps lulled the two as Isabella lifted handful after handful of sand, letting the elements pour through her fingers. Oliver looked at her. His hand drifted to her cheek.

The spirit of love fell anew as their hearts tuned into each other. His eyes caught hers. He could see everything in them. In this transcendent moment, his heart warmed and his mind raced. Isabella knew what was coming. It was just the way she dreamt it would be. They spread across the blanket, and they were one. In these coital moments, they were immortal. In these moments, everything in the world was right, and something deep inside them, unmeasured in spirit, soared unburdened for the first time.

Through the corner of her eye, Isabella saw the scarlet ocean smooth out into a glassy tabletop. There were no waves; everything was still. Isabella took her lips off Oliver's, and directed his gaze out into the wakeless water. "It's just . . . I've never seen the ocean like this. It's so peaceful."

After the sun went down, the sky became a velvet landscape with a waxing moon. The temperature dropped, but the sand around them stayed warm, like their presence was recharging earth's core.

They ended up lying there all night, talking and taking it all in. Oliver looked up at the curtain of blinking stars and whispered, "That's the beauty of the night, Isabella, as dark as it may be sometimes, somewhere in the world, there is light."

She was absorbed in his words and drawn into him. She heard the voice of a boy who had dropped his guard.

The two slept soundly, sharing the same dream.

THE ARCHITECT

SUNRAYS TOASTED OLIVER and Isabella awake. The sky was now more relaxed. It was blue and orange and pink and massively serene. Isabella rolled over and smiled at Oliver on the blanket. Her smile was all he'd ever need.

They made their way back to their lodging and prepared to board the ferry to Barcelona. When they arrived, Oliver and Isabella found Leo alone in the common area, packed. He looked uneasy sitting down with his bag around his shoulders.

Isabella stood to the side of Oliver. "What'd you do with Aisha?"

"Tanning by the beach. That seems to be her thing."

Oliver sharpened his eyes at Leo's tone. Isabella carved up a smile in case her gut was wrong. "Oh, okay . . . great. I'll join her."

She left with visible diffidence.

When the room was only male, Oliver pried. "How'd it go?"

Leo stood. "This whole idea of adventure, I don't think I'm up for it after all. When we get back to mainland, I'm heading home. You do what you want, and I hope you find what you're looking for, but I'm out. I miss home." Leo had evasive eyes. He said nothing more.

Oliver couldn't muster words to reason with his friend. All he managed to say was, "If you want, we can meet you downstairs after we pack up."

Leo nodded and left. The sound of the door shutting was as loud as a bomb.

Oliver was stiff as he fell to the couch. He sat and stared at the rotating fan blade on the ceiling, trying to piece together what happened. Bitter stabs of reproach came as he felt the pendulum of his journey shift.

When the girls returned and Aisha began to pack, Isabella whispered to Oliver, "I didn't learn much, but I guess she and Leo don't feel the way we do."

Oliver caught the vulnerability in these words. "It's too bad they failed." He held her hand. "But I'm glad we didn't."

With everyone packed, they took the ferry home. The ride was uncomfortable. The boys stood outside and leaned against the railing while the girls took seats indoors. While Isabella comforted Aisha, she couldn't help but replay an earlier conversation she had with Oliver.

He had asked her, "How will you explain us to your parents?"

And she had replied, "What do you think I should say?"

"Just that you've met a handsome boy from Spain who is taking time to travel and seeing the world. Right?"

"Well, I think that should work," she said with a hint of sarcasm.

Oliver had taken a stern tone. "Look, Isabella, there's instinct with these things. We just have to go for it."

Isabella had nodded and hidden her concerns. She shied away from telling Oliver about her parents, and was surprised how secretive she had been with him. She trusted Oliver, but maybe not enough—not yet. Or maybe she was just hopeful that things would work out.

Either way, that was the first time the young couple felt a snake of tension between them, and it was unsettling.

When the ferry arrived and they were all ashore, Leo gave his goodbyes and turned towards home. Cut ties were forgotten, and time moved on. Not once did they revive their sundered bond. Leo was a memoir.

A week later, Isabella popped up next to Oliver in her bed. The phone was buzzing. She leaned over and picked it up. Her face immediately went tense. The conversation was brief, and when she hung up, she leapt out from the covers.

"Oliver! You need to get out of here. My parents are coming home early. I'm going to shower. Call Aisha and ask her to come help me clean up. Go to *La Codina* and get a room." Isabella threw the phone to Oliver and jolted into the bathroom. She came out with a toothbrush moving in her mouth, speaking through the suds. "Get your stuff from the guest house. Call me from the hotel."

Oliver parked the Vespa in front of *La Codina*. He dropped his pack at the front desk and slid his identification and money across the marble. Keys came back.

Isabella called shortly after. She and Aisha planned to be away from the house when her parents arrived, but they had to be back for lunch. Oliver was to come.

As Oliver rounded the corner into the lobby, Isabella was whispering on a daybed. "He's a good one, and good ones are supposed to meet the family. I think he'll pass. Don't you?"

Isabella—seeing a pair of feet edging into the lobby—quickly clipped her dialogue. And when she saw Oliver's face, her worries vanished. She felt a new wave of affection for him. If the bellhop had walked over and told her that she wouldn't see Oliver after this, she wouldn't have been able to bear it.

But Oliver didn't share her optimism. This was the first time he felt strange about meeting her parents. All in the lobby, the three anxiously looked at each other before Isabella said, "Here we go. Time for lunch."

Isabella's mother was perfectly dressed as she primly glided down the curved staircase before opening the front door to retrieve the paper.

It was clear where Isabella inherited her beauty; her mother was vital and ageless, and in her face were the memories of wonderful things. Her hair was dark and fell to the middle of her back, and her eyes were clear, like a wreath of starlight. Her physique was slim and weightless, yet she came across with the power of a falcon. At any moment she might take off in flight.

Sofia was delighted to find her daughter prancing up the lowest lawn with Aisha. *But who is the boy?* When the group reached the last line of wind-twisted cypresses, Sofia called out with joy. "Isabella! I thought you'd be home when we got back. It's so good to see you!"

Sofia cheek-kissed Isabella, greeted Aisha, then turned to Oliver and allowed Isabella to introduce them.

"Mother, this is Oliver. I've known him since we lived near Cantabria. He's in town traveling and I happened to run into him. Aisha and I have been showing him around."

Oliver slightly bowed and gave a formal Spanish greeting, but he could tell his presence hit a nerve. Sofia warmed for a moment. "The world is full of surprises. Very nice to meet you, Oliver. Please, call me Sofia."

Oliver smiled, and decided he'd wait a decent interval before calling her by name.

"Where's Antonio, Mom?"

Sofia directed the group's attention down the lawn and out onto the water. "Doing the usual." In the middle of the blue lake, a man dove off his sailboat into the water.

Everyone then turned and entered the house.

Oliver was careful to avoid any indication that he had been here before. They all made way to the sunroom for breakfast, where Sofia set the newspaper under the patriarch's plate. She sat and looked at her daughter. "Okay, Isabella. Tell me everything!"

And Isabella did. And while she did, everyone ate. Isabella seamlessly told of the last few weeks while marshalling the message of romance. Sofia then highlighted their trip to Italy and spoke of how she envisioned getting a summer home there one day.

As Sofia was finishing, Isabella's stepfather, Antonio, came in. Antonio had hawk eyes and a bloodhound nose. He wore five-inch floral trunks, a half-buttoned linen shirt, and atop his rectangular head was a mane of black hair. Antonio had an athletic body gone soft, browned skin, and a salt-and-pepper beard. His light blue eyes glowed when he saw his stepdaughter.

"Isabella!"

As he embraced her he eyeballed the room. A scornful and dismissive look etched across Antonio's face as he issued Oliver a subdued hello. Antonio wasn't really looking for a response, so Oliver nodded back as sweat dripped down his spine. He had hoped that he and Antonio might agree on philosophy or politics or even pop culture, but he could sense that he and the architect were in no way similar people.

Antonio took his chair and loaded his plate propped up by the paper. Sofia took her time to recite the stories which had just been given to her, and she did so with remarkable detail. The others aided her along with interlaced handfuls of polite nothings, and as they did, Oliver studied Antonio's face. It told him nothing. The architect concealed his thoughts like a master of facial features; his disposition was like a palate of hardened mortar.

Everything was fine until Sofia dropped in a theory that Isabella and Oliver were "together." Hearing this, Antonio coughed on his drink as he tried not to choke on this kidney stone of information.

Blood darkened his forehead, and suddenly, the newspaper was sizzling under his plate. Antonio burned with desire to pick it up and mull over the news. *What difference would it make if I address it now or later?* he thought. Antonio burned. He burned until the thought occurred that not lifting the news from under his plate might send him into cardiac arrest, so he did.

He yanked it up to his face. Food tumbled onto the table. He took his left ankle and set it above his right knee while shifting his hips. He sat like the stud he was and scanned the left panel of news summaries in silence. No one spoke.

Finally, he looked up with an iron smile and excused himself and Isabella out to the garden. As Isabella closed the sliding door, she found Oliver's eyes through the glass. All the optimism they had built up plummeted.

Antonio was a protector. He watched over his stepdaughter with a careful eye. And as good fathers do, he found it hard to accept that Isabella was growing up, and that boys viewed her as charming, and fun, and lovely.

Pacing in his garden, Antonio had a tough time with this, so he pushed back on the irrational script that is puppy love, questioning her decision to bring the boy home.

"I'm not going to be around forever, Isabella. I just want to make sure you're taken care of, that you're provided for, that you are treated the way you deserve."

"But . . . I've fallen for Oliver! I've known him for so long. He's not just a random boy."

Antonio dismissed the possibility. He had seen this false pretense before; he'd seen friends rush into relationships they weren't ready to handle. "Isabella, here's what I fear will happen. You two may stay together and even marry young. You'd live peacefully for a few years and be happy for that time and you'd find comfort in the steadiness and calmness that untested love brings. But there is an itch, Isabella, a natural, biological itch in men that women cannot scratch. It has nothing to do with you. It's just something built into us, like a flaw. We are reckless at heart. We have to let the savage in us breathe before we can genuinely settle down."

Antonio continued pacing. "Even for me, Isabella. It took me time to mature. And this boy is not there yet. He longs to see the world, to find danger, to roam free. And if he ends his journey here, at some point he will be so consumed by the possibility of 'what if' that it will tear you two apart. I fear that eventually he will grow unhappy, and you'll regret having asked him to stay."

"But how do you *know* this is the right decision?"

"Because, Isabella, I can hear it in his words, see it on his face, and feel it in my stomach. You have to trust me. I'm just trying to look out for you."

She looked at the ground, defeated. "It's just sometimes I feel so trapped."

"If you two really are meant for each other, one day he will return." Antonio hugged her deeply, trying to absorb her anguish.

Isabella took Antonio's advice with solace. She understood that most things in life are exciting in the beginning but quickly lose their luster. If Oliver was the one, they would meet again. One day.

With an empty spirit, Oliver thanked Sofia for the meal, shook hands with Antonio, and hugged the girls. Oliver was full of cheap glory as he withdrew from the grounds down the succession of terraced lawns, and away from love.

When the stars hung over the water that night, Oliver snuck back to Isabella's home. The young couple wanted to see each other one last time, so they had agreed to meet in the pink-caper garden under the moonlight.

When they met, Isabella held back, but there was still unmistakable electricity passing between them. Oliver gently stroked her hairline. As he moved away, Oliver thought he saw something sapphire flicker in her eyes. The blue flash flew across only for a second, but it was long enough for him to see it.

He turned and descended the lawns as a cold shudder passed through him. The moon and the stars blackened and the darkness of the night swallowed him.

In a fateful way, Oliver lost his heart that night.

THE BEL ÉTAGE

OLIVER WAS BACK in the Bel Étage, standing in front of the lacquered bar. Behind the countertop, a groomed man with metallic blue eyes and a starched shirt was polishing the wooden surface. The bartender didn't give any notice to Oliver or the man he was with.

Around Oliver's neck was a seven-fold tie and beneath that a virile suit. In his hand was a black umbrella that was folded in and soaking wet, which was unusual, as they were indoors.

Oliver glanced at his wristwatch. It wasn't working. He checked again, staring at the second-hand for a few moments. There was no movement. The watch was dead. Something was off here, as if Oliver had crossed an invisible line into a place he never dreamt he'd come.

Oliver set the umbrella across a stool and took a seat. The man with him did the same. Seeing this, the bartender nodded and began mixing ingredients into a shaker. Oliver leaned forward on the bar and put his hand to his jawline. It was bristly and scruffy. He could feel the age on his face—life was beginning to weight him down.

"Time is harsh, Oliver. It doesn't give you a chance to go back and fix a mistake. So, to cope, your mind creates a gossamer of regeneration to convince itself that everything will be alright. But the mind cannot fool the soul . . . and deep in your gut, you know that it may not be. This is a battle we all face. We are forced to balance our physical world and our shared reality with an abstract universe of unknown creation. So, no matter how far the tides of time wash our minds away from our actions, a splinter of regret will always remain lodged within us. When you left Isabella, your mind was forced to create the pain you experienced. But the cosmos is speaking to you . . . it wants to help you heal your heart."

Suddenly, Oliver was very aware of the rapid beating in his chest. He turned to respond to the man sitting next to him, and when he did, Oliver again caught the eyes of the horologist. Black pearls of hematite for the pupils. Filmy conceptions beneath. And where a strained, red vein might diverge like a river system, there was order. The whiteness of his eyes was layered over something. It wasn't clear if the markings originated above or below, but the grid was like a matrix of double-helixes. The horologist had the DNA of something metaphysical. Oliver widened his mouth and led with his index finger. "You're the horologist? Weren't we over—"

With a look of incomprehension, Oliver rotated from the bar to the restaurant. The dining room was now scarred and dilapidated by the acoustics of time. The walls, scorched by heat. The piano was not sleek and raven but coated with an antique dust. The door at the top of the staircase was now stone and Paleolithic, like the entrance to a tomb.

The mammoth glass window looked out to an unbroken expanse of sand dunes and a dead, grey sky. Oliver watched as a turret of wind took a dune and smashed it into the ground. Like the toppling of a domino, this first gust swirled up into a raging storm, generating waves of static over the wasteland. The sky crackled as low peals of thunder roared and beaded lightning illuminated the tundra. The land beyond was of bleached bone—a ruin more ancient than Egypt and more bloodless than a sand pit.

Oliver returned his focus inside. He stared at the floor of the restaurant and noticed a rectangular patch of moonlight shining in from above. Through a hole in the ceiling, he could see a full moon. The violet-black moonlight trickled in and gave the Bel Étage a mauve, surreal distinctness.

No one in the restaurant behaved any differently. The servers were bustling, the diners were feasting, and the attendants were chaperoning the affair. Oliver began to panic.

Time decelerated as his heartbeat grew louder and a swell of silence filled the restaurant. Every person in the dining room stopped what they were doing and stared at Oliver, like each and every unrelated conversation came to the same pause. The stillness was suffocating.

Relief washed over him when the horologist answered. "Yes, Oliver, I'm the horologist. We've met once before. The décor. You must be wondering—"

"Is this really the same place?"

"Define place, Oliver. Is a place physical? Or is a place simply the brain's interaction with its surroundings?" The horologist spoke in concepts and fusillades of the earliest ideas in history. "Places are defined by our perception of them. So, in a way, where we are right now, is really just a reflection of you."

The bartender walked over and set down a pair of clear martinis with a gaseous, sapphire vapor swirling from the brim like dry ice. The horologist plucked one from the bar and took a sip.

Oliver did the same, taking a long slug to clear his head. The bouquet rippled up his nose and the liquid rolled over his tongue. Each sip was satisfying, but not a single drop emptied from the drink. The horologist resumed. "At some point in life, love gets taken from us all. In fact, the loss of love is what kills everyone in the end. Because without it, we feel rotten, we feel like there's poison eating us from the inside, drying us out, making us desolate and hollow. So, you see, Oliver, this is exactly what I've been trying to fix, because lost love is the one thing which time can never heal."

Just then, a weight dropped into Oliver's breast pocket. Transcendentalism exposed the arcane as he withdrew the alloy pocket watch. It had not been there before. Oliver held the clock, feeling its weight and power in his hand, and gradually, his brain became aware of what he was seeing.

"Time has exquisite things in store for you, Oliver. Then again, time has exquisite things in store for us all."

Oliver brushed his fingers over the crafted trinket of synchronicity. He felt like he could fold the world in half; like he had a grip on the constellations.

The horologist whispered, "Oliver. This is yours. This is your time. I make one for every life, but few get to see my design. You have been brought here for a reason, and I believe that reason is important. Oliver, if one life were to be lived fully and completely, giving form to every feeling, expressing every thought, realizing every dream, the world would gain such a fresh impulse of what life is that people would unwind from their habit of not living. Fortunately, the direction of the world can be altered with one oar. And I believe that oar, Oliver, is you, but your clock is ticking."

Oliver took another slug of the martini. "How will I know where to row?"

"Don't worry about that. Just be yourself. That alone is a challenge in our world that tries to make you someone else. Things will happen when they are meant to. Just remember what I told you. Besides, I'll be around."

The rest of the drink was fog to your protagonist.

THE CLOTHIER

TWO MONTHS CRAWLED along as Oliver and Isabella learned to once again live without each other.

Isabella missed Oliver terribly. She missed his charm, his humor, his pride. She missed him holding her. She daydreamed, and imagined him coming back in a mirage of passion, of poetry, of vigor. And she told herself that she would wait.

Oliver felt contrite, he felt rueful, forlorn and cleaved. He had been swept up by the euphoric wave of love only to be flattened by the patriarchal hand of doubt. He felt like Cupid's evil twin had sprayed petrol over his ribs, rubbed gunpowder across his sternum, and blown the cage.

His heart hung open, exposed like a fresh wound. It sat there shriveled, delicate in its beating. Oliver had lent it out and made himself vulnerable, and all that came back was pain.

Oliver went north after Barcelona, and in eastern France his Vespa died. He hiked into the nearest town as the sun was setting, and found the local mechanic drunk at a pub. After listening to the boy's determined plea, the mechanic finally agreed to tow the scooter into his garage that night. Oliver watched the mechanic sway in his steps as he led them to his grimy truck. The mechanic's eyes glossed over while he choked the engine on and set it in gear. The moon was only a sliver that night and the headlights of the tow were dull and dim. Everything about the ride made Oliver uneasy, and when they arrived at the Vespa, his gut had been right.

As the tow approached, the truck began to veer off the lip of the road. Oliver cried out at the mechanic, whose chin was resting on the wheel. The mechanic reacted too late and the pickup plowed into the scooter like a grenade. The Vespa crunched and folded in; it bounced across the dirt road and ripped apart in a symphony of grinding. The collision took Oliver into the glove box, and the contents of his pack spilt all over the truck cabin. Then everything went quiet.

The violence of the incident sobered the mechanic, and seeing the wreckage, his blood boiled and animosity tightened his face. Then came screams, and threats. The mechanic's eyes blew up like bottle rockets as he beefed himself up and warned Oliver that he was not to return to the town—or else. The mechanic was wrathful as he kicked Oliver out into the night and threw his open pack out behind him. The tow turned and drove off.

Lying on the road, Oliver lifted a strand of hair from his forehead and watched the somber beams of the pickup punch through the night. He felt a million miles away from earth. *How could this happen? What did I do to deserve this?* He stood, hitched his pants, brushed his shirt, and gathered his pack.

The money. He couldn't find the envelope. He turned out his pack and raced his hands across his body. "No. No!" It wasn't there. The envelope his parents gave him must have fallen out in the cab.

Oliver whimpered. He missed home. He missed his parents. *Should*

I call and admit I can't make it on my own? Oliver felt cold with shame. The world seemed to be at its darkest.

He looked up to the night sky. A string of flickering light was etching its way across the canopy of stars. It was almost blinding. Oliver watched until it faded into the ether. The bright energy seemed to cleanse him. It reminded Oliver how brief life is, and how much he still had to do. The sensation dwarfed his troubles. He thought of the universe and its unfathomable distance, and he began to find himself happy.

In this moment, Oliver realized that all he would ever want was the means to provide for the people he cared for, and to give back to the people and the world who had given him so much. It wasn't clear how he would get where he was going, nor where his final destination would be, but somehow he knew he was going to make it.

Oliver put his feet in front of him, looked down an unknown road, and began to walk. There was no reason to stop. Distance is nothing when one has motive.

Besides, not everyone who wanders is lost.

Dawn neared when Oliver reached the next town. Cars and trucks had passed him on the road, but he hadn't been in the mood to ride. He was exhausted, but he didn't have money, so he headed for the fields. On the backside of a hill, he found comfort under a beech tree as the stars began to wane. Oliver placed his pack beneath his head and used it as a pillow. He smiled at the simplicity of the world. He had nothing, yet, for the first time since he left Barcelona, it felt like he had everything. As his eyes shut against his pack, he thought, *Sometimes, we forget all that we have.*

Oliver stirred to a fresh day. The pasture around him was full of cattle, and for the first moments he had to remember how he got to where he was. He yawned, then began to laugh. Not a merry laugh but a painful laugh, like when your leg is asleep. It was a mix of anguish and irrational faith. Adversity had come, and it had come unfriendly, and vicious; sharp and incisive like a predator with an open snout. Oliver knew that one day he would look back and cherish this interval, but inside the moment, life was notably queer.

Oliver gathered himself. He checked once more for the money. Still not there. He laughed that painful laugh, then headed into society. He had passed through this town on the road and remembered seeing a market near the center.

When he arrived, Oliver edged through the rows of vendors and stands. The exchange was surprisingly quiet, and as he slowly moved through, he could feel the yellow, depraved eyes of the vendors crawling all over his body. They stayed in the shadows of their stands, whispering and dispersing behind their piles of inventory, looking at Oliver like a toothsome steak. Each breath he took seemed to sing out like an explosion. The suspense crushed him; he had no idea what to do. *Should I beg? Should I ask for food or water or money? Should I try to find a ride home?*

Oliver continued to move along. He found himself timid and fearful. His pride failed him even though he was hungry and thirsty and couldn't have felt more vulnerable if he had leprosy or wore a sign across his chest with big red letters reading, *Help!*

That night, he went hungry. He returned to the beech tree as darkness flapped like a black wing, and Oliver had a dream that his mother wandered over the hill to save him.

The next day, things changed when Oliver came to a bird pen in the market. The gate was open. He studied the birds and wondered why they stayed in the cage when freedom was so near. He watched as they hopped on their pencil legs and pecked at the feed. Maybe they were born in captivity, and just didn't know they could fly. Maybe it would just take one bird, to show the rest the way.

Oliver stepped back from the pen. He looked around for the owner, but couldn't tell who it was, so he called to the people nearby. Suddenly, as he spoke, Oliver was very aware of his rugged his appearance and the dirt on his face. It had been a long stretch since he showered.

On cue, the owner of the terrarium rushed over to shut the gate, and while he did, the bird closest to the exit leapt up to the wiry ledge, poked its beak out, and soared. Swiftly, the scent of freedom spread, and the entire pen began to empty from the cage, ascending in an organized wave and disappearing.

The owner was fuming as he gaped at his empty lot. "A month of rent. Gone! Why didn't you shut the gate? You cost me—"

Oliver stared at nothing. He felt very small as he began to armor himself against the horrors that surely awaited. The man before him was insane, tears boiling from his red eyes. In the archives of his mind, Oliver plowed through shelves looking for some petition, some supplication, some way to escape this man's wrath.

"Perhaps the owner should have been more responsible." This voice came from behind Oliver.

The veins in the bird-keeper's forehead enlarged into gyrating worms. He yelled back, "Gabriel! Mind your business!"

"Oh, I assure you, if anyone was ever doing so, it was I." Oliver twisted around to see a middle-aged man dressed in the height of fashion. He was adding needles to a foam orb on his wrist. He had a forehead wide rather than high, dark clustering hair, and a strong chin, maybe a bit too strong for his face. He stood from his booth and glided over to protect Oliver like a father does a child.

"It is a pity when a grow man refuses to take responsibility." Gabriel spoke to the bird owner: "I'll see him out."

Oliver and his protector withdrew from the market.

"You have to be careful roaming around here. Many of these people are fond of protecting a dignity they never had, and your accuser is one of them. I saw you here yesterday. Why are you slewing around by yourself?" Gabriel said calmly.

"I'm kind of lost."

"Temporarily. I bet you could use some rest. Come along and we'll figure out how to get you back on track."

As they walked, Oliver explained how he ventured from home, met a wonderful musician and a beautiful girl, and how things had gone awry since. Oliver's dirty appearance didn't inspire confidence, but the strength in the boy's face told Gabriel a different story—one of determination.

Finally, Oliver asked, "What is it that you do?"

"I help give people an image."

Gabriel led Oliver to his shop. As he unlocked the door, Oliver examined two mannequins dressed in dapper suits in the front window. In the entry of the studio, a pair of blue-leather easy chairs sat beside a matching end table. The rest of the shop was lined with elegantly designed menswear. Gabriel gestured for Oliver to take a seat.

"I suppose I don't have the right to ask, but where are you headed next? And how will you get there?"

Oliver shrugged. He didn't have an answer.

"How would you like to work in my shop for a while? Just to get back on your feet,"

Oliver phoned home and told his parents the news. He told them how he got a job and how he was still excited to see the world, and find his purpose, and become someone. He told them that his tailoring duties were temporary and that he would be back on the road soon, and he would even stop by if he came their way. There had been a wrinkle of doubt in their voices, but his parents were proud of their son's perseverance and offered their support if he needed it.

Things at Gabriel's shop started slow. The first shirt took Oliver five days of practice. As time passed, five days turned to three, and three days to one, and finally Oliver felt he was ready to thread his first suit.

"Your first assignment," Gabriel said, holding up a navy jacket, "is to sew your own suit. It can be your uniform at the shop."

As time went on, Gabriel continued to be impressed by Oliver; he hadn't expected such drive in the boy. Oliver knew that work was never something to complain about or make excuses for. Work was how he could prove himself, and what would ultimately provide him with the resources to continue his journey to find fulfillment. Oliver outworked Gabriel, and he did it by dint of his own grit. In this way, in hard work and sincere effort, Oliver created a foundation on which he could build his cairn.

With each suit that Oliver stitched, the harshness of the past withered, and before he knew it, a year passed in the clothier's shop. Isabella, Antonio, Leo, and everything else seemed a lifetime ago.

"I was thirteen when my brother got married. As a groomsman, I had a tuxedo fit for me. I watched the tailor mold the fabric to my frame, and I saw the joy he had while doing it. It may sound cliché, Oliver, but ever since that fitting, I wanted to become a clothier myself."

Gabriel was still speaking when a man let the shop door close. The entrant had high cheekbones and an avian nose, an Adam's apple that bobbed when he spoke, and a mossy brown comb-over. He strolled over with a grin and open arms. "Gabriel. So good to see you."

The clothier returned the embrace, then the entrant made his way to the blue easy chairs and opened a magazine he carried under his arm. Oliver glanced at the spread, where on the cover, a headshot of a man with vulpine good looks and crystal-white eyes stared back. Under his invincible chin in large white letters it read, *New York Real Estate Tycoon Takes the UK.*

Oliver would not forget that face.

Gabriel continued speaking while he examined the record book. "With practice, Oliver, I dovetailed into a practice of my own, then began to design my own clothing line."

Gabriel went to the back of the shop and pulled a cream-colored suit, tan shirt, and a sapphire tie for the entrant.

The customer returned to the parlor fully dressed, looking like he was about to attend a polo match. He stood before the three-mirrored podium, and caught eyes with the clothier as he unwound his measuring tape. "Did anyone ever doubt you, Gabriel? Going off on your own? Focusing on clothes rather than school?"

"Of course, Mr. vom Glas, of course. You know the story. My parents nearly cast me out when I decided to not attend college."

Gabriel checked all the measurements while speaking. "As time passes, people start to believe that they can't reach their goals, and they unintentionally pass on their disbeliefs, telling people things like, 'You can't do that,' or 'It'll never work.' You just have to decide for yourself whether you believe in something or not."

"Very true, Gabriel. So, why didn't you quit?"

"Simple. I love doing what I do. That's what gets you through all the negativity and doubt."

"I couldn't agree more." Mr. vom Glas motioned for Oliver to move closer and spoke primarily to him. "Make sure you enjoy yourself no matter what you do. Then learn from those who have already carved great paths, so that even if you don't reach their height, you will at least yield some of their scent. Do like prudent archers who, the place where they intend to shoot seeming too far, aim much higher than their target."

The garments fit exactly as requested. Mr. vom Glas began removing his tie and coat. "Imagine yourself as that archer. You're standing in front of an apple orchard. There are rows of trees before you, and on the closest tree line are juicy pieces of fruit just waiting to be struck. But before you set your aim, you scan the range once more, and you see it off in the distance. You're sure it's there, but not how far it is or how much it's worth. What you see is the golden apple. And you look at your fellow archers standing to your left and your right and realize that they can all see the golden apple too. It's sitting there dormant at the top of the orchard.

"Now, you'd think that everyone would at least try and take a shot at the prize, but the reality is that 99 percent of your peers will aim for the low-hanging fruit out of fear or practicality. The golden apple may seem impossibly out of reach and ridiculous to expect, but that's why it remains—because so few take the shot."

Mr. vom Glas cleared his throat.

"What your peers won't realize is that they can fail to hit the low-hanging fruit too. So why not take a chance to strike gold? Society will tell you that the golden apple is beyond your aim and out of reach, and that your fellow archers fared well with the easy shot. But ask yourself this: If you can see the prize in the distance, how long until another archer plucks it from its perch? And even if you miss on your first try, who is to say that you are only allotted one arrow? That's nonsense. Shoot for the golden apple, and if you miss, don't reverse course and settle for the low fruit. Realize the tremendous advantage you have after failing. Missing with your first arrow lends insight into the correct trajectory. You learn from your risks, and this allows you to feel more confident as you take your next shot. As long as you are willing to let your hunger drive you beyond the grit of others, the golden apple is yours for the taking."

Gabriel chimed, "Yes, Mr. vom Glas! Never let the probability of success justify the effort."

Mr. vom Glas withdrew from the main room. And as he did, Gabriel developed a notion. *Mr. vom Glas is a golden apple.* His grandfather was a famous businessman who had brought economic and political stability to his country. Mr. vom Glas, born into wellness, was an heir.

Gabriel excused himself to the back. Oliver heard muted murmuring before the two men emerged. Mr. vom Glas approached Oliver, back in his original clothes.

"Oliver, Gabriel told me your story. It's inspiring. He has wonderful things about you: that you hold a pureness of heart, and an unteachable work ethic. What would you think about coming with me to Luxembourg for a little while? No strings attached, right Gabriel?"

The clothier smiled. It was time.

THE HEIR

A BUG-EYED SUV rolled up in front of the clothier's shop. The exterior of the vehicle was a light, misty green with black expedition wheels and a tan clamshell roof. Daniel tossed open his door and edged around the trunk looking like a lumberjack. He had a bushy beard and a head of rolling, mocha hair. His eyes were brown, a deep, black-coffee brown, and he wore a red, wool sweater coat with tribal patterns. His sleeves gripped tight around his forearms, and he had legs that could uproot a tree. But overall, his demeanor was soothing and jovial, and reflective of a rich inner life.

When he rounded the vehicle, Daniel was surprised to find his uncle walking out with a young accomplice. Daniel gave a proximate hello, then tossed open the trunk of the SUV. One of the doors fell into a tailboard and the other reached for the clouds as it hydraulically propelled upward.

When everything was loaded and they were rolling away, Oliver felt a burning sensation in his chest. He was moving farther and farther from home, and for the first time in a long while, the thought of Isabella trickled into his mind.

He had once believed that he loved Isabella. But had he been in love, or was it all a trick? After he had left Barcelona, he told himself the best thing to do was to forget about her, and he had. And, once again, embracing a new road on the adventure of life, he did . . . and the fire within him withered until there was only one little ember that remained, one little piece of warmth that sat idle in his soul.

An hour later, the SUV approached the suburbs of Luxembourg. In a particularly grandiose neighborhood, envy swept through Oliver as he admired the estates. He looked at the window, his forehead almost on the glass. "These people must have such great lives. One day I will have that too."

Mr. vom Glas said, "Oliver, yes, some of those people are very pleased with life, but unfortunately, not all of them are. Some people buy large homes thinking that ten thousand square feet will make them rich, but after they move in, they don't feel satisfied because they're missing something inside themselves. When you feel poor it doesn't matter how big your home is or how many nice things you have to fill it with. You have to search within to find what you are truly looking for."

"I can attest to that, Oliver." Daniel glanced in the rearview mirror, his hands on the wheel. "My wife and I used to have a big place, but after a year living in it, we realized it was only a burden in our lives. So, we sold it along with many of our material possessions. Since then, I've never felt richer or freer. I imagine we'll settle down when we have a little one, but we'll keep the things in our life to a minimum."

Mr. vom Glas picked back up. "Oliver, money is a snide treasure. It can get you almost anything you desire, except the things you desire most." Mr. vom Glas paused and his disposition shifted. "I know this from experience. When I was a working man, I made an assumption about the world and built my life on top of it. I assumed that money could solve my problems, so I chased it relentlessly, and by doing so, I only created more problems in my life and a reputation of lavishness.

Eventually, my wife grew so fed up with me that she took the children and left. She loved me, but she thought I was incurable in my lust. Oliver, allow me to show you a few things during your stay; then I may be able to help broaden your journey."

Oliver agreed, and Daniel continued the drive to Luxembourg.

The square was stirring. Oliver followed Mr. vom Glas as he goosed his way into a stout building with neoclassical columns spread across the front. A fountain gushed inside, and gold moldings lined the lobby. Bankers in three-piece suits drifted atop the marble floor while subtle discussions echoed through the anteroom.

A stylish gentleman strolled over with highly alert eyes. "Good evening, Mr. vom Glas."

"Good evening, Nigel. I'd like to show my friend the vault."

Nigel shuffled out of sight. Mr. vom Glas turned to Oliver and whispered with a wink, "Right on time."

Nigel returned without a key in his hand. "After you, sir."

Mr. vom Glas led the small order through layers of security. They passed corridor after corridor of loan-seekers and corporate clientele, then, without notice, came to a halt in the middle of a deserted corridor. Mr. vom Glas averred, "Here we are. Thank you, Nigel."

He reached out into the bald air and pushed forward. Seemingly out of thin air, the empty hallway opened. Mr. vom Glas steered Oliver into the vault. "An elegant ruse, double-sided glass."

The vault door was nine inches of reinforced steel with mechanized gears and heavy bolts. Once inside, Oliver looked down the bare hallway to see Nigel walking back towards the lobby.

"This is the vault of Luxembourg," Mr. vom Glas orated.

Citadels of lockboxes lined the walls. Oliver and Mr. vom Glas convened at the only table in the depository, an aluminum console with four chairs not meant for leisure. The heir grinned as he watched Oliver blaze around with glossy eyes. "I brought you here to show you that everything you'll ever need is inside this room."

"Well, of course. With all this money, anyone could do anything."

The heir shook his head with affection. "Oliver, the money and jewels in here won't help you. Like I said in the car, it's what's in here." He pointed to Oliver's chest.

Mr. vom Glas spread his arms and tilted his palms up as if he were bearing the weight of the chamber. "If you store your happiness in money, you will never be satisfied, because there will always be an allure to have more. A bank account cannot be filled. There is always room to its add to its size."

"Are you telling me to not seek wealth?"

The heir leaned forward. "First, Oliver, define wealth. Even with all the money in the world, you could be far from wealthy. Money is just an invention; it's a derivative of our economic machine. If you believe money is wealth, you are placing your happiness in numbers, and numbers never end. People think, 'If I had a million dollars, I'd be happy.' But, I promise you, thinking that some number will satisfy you is a recipe for disaster. I can assure you, it won't."

Mr. vom Glas could see sorrow purl across the boy's face, but he kept on. "Oliver, the hard truth is that our culture breeds a mindset of materialism. So many of us are absorbed in egotistical things—titles, houses, cars, furnishings. It's endless. What I've learned—what I'm trying to teach you—is that you should take a step back and look at what *you* want out of life, not what society tells you that you need. Only when you've defined what you value as an individual person can you know what will bring you wealth."

Oliver studied the joy on Mr. vom Glas's face as he taught. He could tell that there was sincere equanimity in these statements. "So, wealth is obtained by setting your own standards and values, and then going into the world and trying to fulfill them?"

Mr. vom Glas nodded, then flipped his wrist to check the time. "Still on schedule. Let me show you what I mean."

They exited back through the marble lobby and out to the square.

It was rush hour. The streets flooded as breadwinners poured out of their offices. Oliver and Mr. vom Glas idly observed the people on their way, all in a feverous hustle.

"Oliver, tell me what do you see."

The boy studied the crowd in detail. The people around him raced by each other with designer briefcases and biting faces. Everyone seemed to be detached and living in separate worlds.

With a hint of discomfort, Oliver replied, "I see clouds, Mr. vom Glas. Not of the sky, but of the mind. I wouldn't have noticed them before. I see all these talented people rushing from one place to the next, but I don't see very much happiness. Maybe I'm missing something."

"What do you mean?"

"It's like people are trapped in their own thoughts. It's seems like they've chosen such vigorous careers of exertion but are still looking for something beyond the money and titles and social prestige. I only hope they know why they choose to do so."

"Unfortunately, Oliver, most people fall into their paths. But it's not them who we must change. Their behavior is an offshoot of a culture where paychecks have become medicine, and careers are not much more than economic prescriptions for vapidity." The heir digressed, "But enough for now. My stomach is rumbling, which means you must be famished, and I know just the place." They vacated the square, dodging the clouds as they went.

Mr. vom Glas wiped his lips and ordered more wine. The kitchen had been closed for an hour and the bar was beginning to shut down when he drove the conversation from small talk.

"So, Oliver, our deal is complete. You've been impressively observant. All I ask is that you don't allow your happiness to hinge on material possession. Well, and also that you don't go around sharing the whereabouts of our vault!" He handed Oliver an envelope with enough to travel for a long time.

"You must have make a mistake, Mr. vom Glas." Oliver had quickly estimated the amount. "This can't be for me."

"I'm quite sure it is, Oliver. I have far too much of that stuff, and I believe that you can use it for good."

"How can I ever repay you?"

"Our time together has been a two-way street. I've learned a lot myself. Although, maybe one day, I'll call on you for assistance. Perhaps nothing more than an ear to bounce ideas off, but maybe more."

"Of course. For what, though?"

"Fixing our culture. Fixing the clouded minds we saw all around us. It may sound odd, Oliver, but I believe the problem is rooted in our school system. Education has become an anesthetic for creativity. It is outdated and meant to mold people into employees, not to nurture free thought. Children are taught a binary curriculum—do this, not that, and this is why. Uniformity has trumped the rebel, and that is a terrible thing."

Oliver thought of his time sitting in class. "I guess school has a predictable outcome, huh?"

"Students are farmed to be full of envy and doubt. Then they go out into the workforce and real world and get stuck in a rut, unhappy and unfulfilled. Education needs to motivate and encourage the youth. It needs to free their minds and nurture creative thought." Mr. vom Glas sipped his wine. "There was a time when standardized education benefitted society much more than it does now. In the age of industrialism, those without jobs could attend school and receive one. That was fast progress then, but the system has been stagnant since."

"So, what will you change?"

"This is where my resources play an advantage. I want to fix society's shortsightedness and reliance on the past. We need leaders, not quarterly profit targets and yearly salary increases. We need visionaries, and visionaries are much rarer to come by in a system where the imagination is suppressed and attention-related disorders are over-diagnosed."

The heir placed his hands over his face. "My wife, my beautiful wife, is the one who taught me all this. She's a professor, and it was her dream to revamp education and pump fresh oxygen into the institution. She always said that the real world is far from standardized, and to teach children otherwise is malign. She said that by teaching our children to think within a box, society misses the opportunities that exist outside the models of academia.

"My wife begged me and pleaded with me to divert my attention away from profit margins and to help her with her mission. But I wouldn't listen. I didn't think it mattered as much as my business. I grew so detached from my family that I stayed late in the office just to avoid them. I failed to be a father, and I failed to be a husband. So, they picked up and left. Now, I have to make things right. It's all I have left."

Oliver pushed his chair away, circled the table, and placed his hand on the heir's back. "You may feel sick today, sir, but that doesn't mean you'll feel that way tomorrow. We mustn't let our past be a sentence for our future."

Mr. vom Glas looked up. He knew he had made his point.

Hours had drifted into the sand. Dusk had fallen, and a volley of mist showered the city. Rain flushed the gutters, and filaments of light dimly glowed, bobbing through the downpour as the drops of rain leapt back up as soon as they hit the street.

Oliver looked outside with an adventurous mind. "I'm going for it; the water will guide me. You don't know how much this has meant to me, Mr. vom Glas. I'll see you again sometime, on this side or the other."

"Be a soldier as you go out into the world, Oliver. We need you. Embrace pain while you rest and exhaust yourself while under no attack, so that when a real test comes, you will have already won. Seek to grow every day, and you may find wealth long before I do."

Oliver then stepped out into the current, and back into uncertainty.

THE SOUS CHEF

OLIVER WAS SURPRISED how cold the air was. It was edging into the eerie part of night, about the time when it seems like there are no rules and the world feels a bit unsafe. The street was mute except for the sound of the black water ricocheting off the pavement. Oliver tossed his jacket on and trotted through the concave avenues of Luxembourg.

Hunches guided his direction as he navigated in a blind canter. Rounding the curve of a wet alley, Oliver came to a pier along a river. Rows of shadowy barges lined the waterway and stacks of shipping containers sat like coffins to the right. Under a post lamp, shipmen in slickers were unloading cargo from a barge. They must have been at it for hours; on top of the dock sat a large pyramid of cedar boxes, the type with stamped red arrows that had been nailed together by heavy industrial equipment.

At the top of the pyramid sat the supervisor. The figure perched just beyond the pool of light, but seemed accessible enough. Oliver sailed across the pier and settled near the outermost crate while the crew continued to unload. With his hands cupped into a bullhorn so his voice could carry through the rain, Oliver called, "Where are you headed?"

The supervisor beyond the light turned and spoke through the drumming water. It was a woman's voice. "Amsterdam. Leavin' momentarily. Wha'd'ya say?"

She then began to climb down from the top. Tied at her waste was a long black raincoat and on her head was a peaked cap. Her neck was a seascape of tattoos, and clutched between her teeth was a hand-rolled cigarette. She was maybe a year older than Oliver. On the pier, she extended her hand.

Oliver took it as the rain pebbled his cheeks. "Amsterdam. Perfect."

She pointed to her barge. "Sure, she could use a lick of paint here and there, but she's reliable as ever. If you're willing to pass over a reasonable sum, we'd be glad to have ya."

Oliver reached into his coat pocket and withdrew several notes from the disintegrating envelope. She rolled the cigarette like a log in her mouth. "Good to have you aboard. Call me Captain. Captain Devin. This is my crew." Her voice sprung in decibel, and all the men in slickers tipped a hat in Oliver's direction. The nearest one plucked the pack off Oliver's shoulder and, like a production line, passed it down the conveyor of shipmen. Captain Devin and Oliver dipped into the grey hull of the barge.

"The door on the right leads to the quarters. The door on the left leads to my operating room. And the door straight ahead leads to the parlor, and the parlor is where we go."

Captain Devin booted the parlor door open and motioned Oliver to a worn circular table in the center of the room. She dipped behind the bar and tossed her raincoat and cap on the wall while they both cleared their faces of mist. Her arms extended the mural of tattoos from her neck in blue-orange ink. "All right. A wicked wassail is on the horizon."

She lined up a dozen square glasses on the counter. "My crew is wrapping up. We set off on the 'morrow." Captain Devin took a murky decanter of what looked like lamp oil, and splashed the glasses full.

As if a bomb detonated, the parlor door burst open and the crew paraded in. They each grabbed a pony off the bar before they enveloped the circular table and their shoulders and elbows collided. Noticing Oliver without a drink, one of the crew yipped, "Look men, we've got ourselves a landlubber." The circle toasted with laughter. "Night's a moonraker. Get you a pony."

Oliver stood to fetch a glass of the lamp oil. There were only three left. One for Oliver, one for Captain Devin, and one for . . . the door swung open again. Tiers of food wheeled in. Behind the cart, a portly, shiny-cheeked fellow waddled along.

"Sous!" A hurrah came from the table as the cart rolled forward.

"Groggy already, are we mates?" The cadet spun towards the bar and tapped glass with Oliver. "Call me Sous. Too young to be a chef, so for now, they call me Sous."

Captain Devin raised her pony from behind the bar. "To the moonraker."

Everyone shot. The swarthy spirit slid down with a biting finish. Then the cart unloaded as platters and basins of food were tossed around the circle in chaos. All the crewmen were in flux as they suspended their faces over their plates, half-sitting, half-standing in a brutish strategy to maximize their intake.

Four minutes passed before the final bite was taken, and in unison, the entire group cooperatively tossed the dishes back onto the rolling cart before Sous kicked the wheels back into the hall, saying, "The toil is done. Time to dine."

He drew behind the bar and revealed a new platter of ponies. As the liquor settled, Oliver looked around in excitement. This was not your quaint, prim dinner party. This was an itemized riot. They proceeded with the booze and delved into anthems and fables, and in true comradery, everyone around the table lent embellished tales to one another. The night kept on and the ponies kept racing until eventually, one-by-one, the crew began to pull themselves out of the parlor room and into a comatose sleep.

The late night pinched into an early morning, which slid into a tardy lunch. Finally, Oliver roused. He opened his eyes and saw white above him. It took a moment for him to realize that he was looking at the ceiling above the parlor table. With a pillow beneath his head and a blanket over his body, stirring awake wasn't too harsh. But the light from outside, the hideously bright light, burned into his skull like a magnifying glass to an ant.

He cleared his throat. There was no moisture; his tongue, a sand viper buried in dust. Oliver rolled over on the table, and this first action, this first wave of brain activity, came down like a splitting axe. Immediately, it was clear that thinking was going to be a bother for the day. He snapped an eyelid shut, and faced the round window in the hull. The river was traipsing by.

With effort, he swung his feet to the floor and fell off the table. He landed with a gimp, and lifted a leg of his boxers to find a plum bruise on his hamstring. How it came about, no one knew. These things just happen when the ponies race.

It took five hours to dress. Then Oliver crawled up to Captain Devin's operating room. The upper deck was a small, glass-encased galley. Oliver looked out at the river and watched the oval ripples crinkle from the stem of the barge, then moved forward so Captain Devin could see him. She gave a quiet welcome.

"You need the good coffee. When it comes to things like this, you don't mess around." She gripped a thermos and poured a mug halfway to the brim with caffeine.

Then came a leather-bound flask. She handed the full cup to Oliver. "A day to Amsterdam."

Captain Devin then rotated back to her carnival-sized steering wheel, looked to the binnacle of her boat and effortlessly navigated the thalweg of the river channel. Her crew was below on the deck, tending to this and that, and broadly being productive. These shipmen must've had guts of iron, because Oliver was battling to keep the stomach acid below his throat.

But the spiked coffee did wonders. Oliver sipped the brew as quickly as the heat would let him, and when the blackness plunged into his gut, a newfound energy peppered his mood.

"Oliver, I know more about living on water than land. My crew and I grew up together, and in grade school, we tested well in insubordination, so we left."

She took a sip directly from the leather-bound flask. "We're partial to the river's current. It's the volatility of water that we like. The sturdiness of land is maddening."

The woody aroma of the coffee swirled up from the mug and refracted off the sunshine daggering in through the glass. Each sip returned a hue to Oliver's face. He asked Captain Devin where home was.

"Caledonia. When we left on our own, we spent a few months on odd jobs until we had saved enough up to buy her." Captain Devin cradled the steering wheel. "So, what really brings you on our ship?"

"Captain, what'll it be this evening?" Sous had slipped up the staircase behind their necks. He had on a black chef toque, short-sleeve coat, and trousers.

Captain Devin thought for a moment, then tossed open a pane in the galley and called down to her crew on the deck. "Men. What'll it be tonight?"

They all stopped their tasks, nodded at each other, and roared, "Stew."

Captain Devin turned inside to Sous. "Stew."

"Stew," Sous repeated, then turned to the kitchen while Captain Devin refaced the deck. Oliver, however, kept his eyes fixed. He didn't know why, but something told him to not turn away. And when Sous shifted back towards the kitchen, on the back of his hat was the butterfly. Its fiery, sapphire wings flapped like a lady fanning herself.

Oliver's coffee mug slipped from his sweaty palm and shattered on the floor. Sous and Captain Devin jumped at the noise and rushed over to help Oliver, who hadn't moved even as the coffee singed his ankles. He was immobilized. His eyes gushed with tears as he watched the butterfly flutter off the back of Sous's hat and o t the glass pane Captain Devin had left open. With the other two focused on the spill, no one else saw the apparition drift out into the wind. And thereby, the poltergeist vanished again.

Oliver's bodily systems came back on. He felt the white-hot numbness of the boiling coffee seething into his skin and he sprang awake with a cry. Sous escorted him downstairs.

Oliver came to on a bottom bunk in the quarters. He fingered the bubbling burn under his bandages, flipped his knees over the floor, stood, and took a deep breath. Woozy, he sat back on the bed a minute.

He sat in silence, and slowly a remnant thought began to stir, as if the butterfly had planted an idea in his mind. *Isabella.* Oliver imagined her sunning next to the pleasant lakeside air. She surely had moved on by now. There would have been many better looking, better educated, better connected young beaus on her tail. She could relax by the pool with Aisha and take her pick. They girls would wear blue-and-white striped bikinis and size up these callers and make them audition. It would all be a breeze, one big soiree.

Oliver thought back to their nights together, to the innocence and confidence which could never come again; to the nights which had been so delightful; to the nights so far away. *How could she still care for me?* It was an impossibility. He was convinced.

Oliver sighed. He took another breath and gathered himself. *What am I even doing here?* He had gotten lucky that Gabriel had taken him in, and won the lotto with Mr. vom Glas, but where was his direction now?

Oliver stood again and moved through the hull to thank Sous. He peeked through a few doors before coming to the kitchen. When Oliver hobbled in, Sous's elbows were immersed in a sink of suds. He dried his arms and checked on the injury. The burns would heal in a week. Sous smiled and joked about Oliver's lack of athleticism, then they both moved on. No big deal.

The whole kitchen was a thick forest of appliances. Sous squatted in front of a cupboard and began rattling around before hurling ingredients over his shoulder. "Catch! Appetizers!"

Oliver tagged the ingredients from the air and set them on the island counter. When Sous finished, he shuffled over to doctor up a dish. Like a surgeon in the operating room, he took fantastic care as he spruced up his model appetizer.

"A *croque monsieur, wah-lah!*"

He gestured to the large basin of stew on the stove. "Now, I must tend to our entrée—free-range rabbit with lemongrass broth. It will follow your dish nicely." He dipped a ladle in the nascent bouillon and began educating Oliver on his work. "The secret to cooking is olfactory, it's the nose. The smell sets up the taste. So, I will deliver the smell, you deliver the taste."

Oliver turned to the island. Sous's model dish stared right back.

With one eye on the cauldron, Sous coached Oliver, "Make a few trials and eat them yourself. When you are full, start the real ones. It's the only way to practice!"

Sous pointed around the kitchen. "My ingredients are everything. At each stop along the water, I try to head into town and find a fresh farmer's market. The purer the ingredients, the better the food!"

Sous nurtured his entree, tossing in seasonings and shortenings with exactitude. He then began concocting a tomatillo sauce to lay over his side dish of glazed sweet potatoes. And when the sauce was complete, he handwrote the night's menu, orating as he went along, "The subtlest difference between an elegant meal and that of a savage is the menu."

Oliver had just completed his last trial appetizer. He was preoccupied. His mind raced thinking about the sapphire butterfly. He was sure he'd come across it before, but then again, maybe not.

Maybe it was all in his head. No one else had ever caught a glimpse, but still, there was something there. Fear overtook Oliver as he imagined confessing the phantom to someone. *Would I not come across as crazy?*

He buried the idea and returned to the task at hand.

Sous frolicked around his laboratory. "Once a week, Captain Devin and the crew let me keep them mannered. The other six nights are all-out wars for plate space."

Sous then prepared dessert; a simple raspberry tart. He nestled a piece of vanilla-bean sorbet to the side of the tart. "Desserts, when exquisite, are the consummation of all that is delicious."

Sous and Oliver took the remainder of the day to set up the banquet. That evening, the entire affair was proper and relaxing. Each crewmember dressed substantially nicer and seated themselves before the stemware with napkins in their laps. Sous commenced the meal. "Well friends, dig in."

Captain Devin addressed Oliver. "It's been a pleasure. 'Morrow we reach Amsterdam. And we wish you all the best."

Then the ponies raced.

THE BULLDOG

THE NEW YEAR was only hours away.

Bram had already eaten dinner, but the savory aroma coming from the café made him salivate. He sat down along a canal in Amsterdam, then sent for a helping of fish and chips and started on his fourth drink of the night. When the food arrived, Bram's tongue flopped out of his baggy jowls like a bulldog. Slop and drool flew on the table as he emptied the entire tray then fell back in his chair. Bram then lobbed his tongue above his lips and dragged a piece of cod out of his moustache.

"Another drink, miss." He was rattling the ice around his glass when a soft-faced, russet-haired boy walked up and settled in across the patio.

Oliver was beginning to get tired of walking and not really having anything to do, so he sat down at a café along the canal. He fumbled through his pack and once or twice peeped at his watch to check the time, but mainly he considered where to head next as he sat there awaiting midnight. As he sipped an apricot-colored Bellini, Oliver could feel a heavy set of eyes on him.

When he glanced up, what he saw baffled him. His spectator was a hairy bulldog man who had squeezed himself into a stone-colored jacket and matching fedora. When Oliver's eyes met his, the bulldog straightened up, and removed his hat with a wooly forearm to wipe the sweat from his balding head, doing so slowly and solemnly, as if this action was the most important thing he had done all year. Oliver crumpled his face at the sight and turned back towards his table.

When Bram heard Oliver order another drink, it was over before it began. Bram barked across the café, "You might consider Pimm's, boy. It's my personal favorite for the holiday."

Oliver looked up with a gruff face and an uninviting tone. "I'm under the spell of peach schnapps right now . . . but thanks."

Bram plucked his Pimm's off the table and wobbled over. "For this time of year, it's splendid to have such a day."

He of course, was referring to the weather. *The weather! How do I escape this conversation?* thought Oliver, not eager to have uninvited company.

The bulldog took a seat beside Oliver. "Since we're on the subject, you should hear my theory about why everyone talks about the weather when they have nothing better to say."

Oliver finished his second Bellini and listened to his intruder's unabridged monologue about the weather. When Bram stopped, he pulled his head back with a puzzled look.

"You know, dear boy, I must ask. *Who* are you?"

"Sometimes I hardly know."

Bram swirled a spoon through his Pimm's, then lifted an eyebrow. "Oh—and how is that? Doesn't everyone know who they are?"

"Somedays I think I do, and others I don't. The new year always makes me question myself. I can tell you who I was last year, but I have no idea who I'll turn into this one."

Bram pointed his paw to the pedestrians moving along the canal.

"Do you think these people know who they are?"

Oliver shrugged. "I guess not."

Bram was flustered by this. For his whole life, Bram had thought everyone knew themselves, yet this boy was saying the opposite. He sucked through his straw like it was the last noodle of spaghetti on earth. "Look here, boy. People must know who they are. How else would they go about their day?"

Oliver began to grow unpleasant. "Is this all you've come over to say?"

"Why! Keep your temper, young man. Do you think you're above *me*!?" Bram had swelled up in his chair. Bubbles brewed in his Pimm's. "Let me tell you something . . . the fastest way to analyze someone's intellect is to assess the people around them. You are alone, on a holiday. What does that tell me about you then?"

"Don't you have something better to do than attack me!" There was concern in Oliver's voice. "*You* are alone too, you know."

"No, I'm not! I'm with you."

Bram's words seemed to shock them both. Oliver and the bulldog leaned back in their chairs and looked at each other with inebriated eyes, realizing that they were ruining each other's holiday. Bram coughed to open his throat. "I believe we've started off on the wrong foot, my boy. We built a wall between us . . . let us turn that into a door."

He then ordered a new round and offered to cover the bill.

The two drank until the sunlight receded, when the serene black sky shuttered against quick flashes of light. Fireworks, bold in color and eruption, sparkled in the night.

"Perspectives, perspectives." Bram's multi-chin stretched into a gullet as he looked up. Both he and Oliver were sufficiently intoxicated now. "It's easy to forget about all the marginal events that happen outside of view . . . the things we don't see. Yes, the fireworks are beautiful, but think of how wonderful the performance is on the launch pad, of the orchestration and the precision of the operating team. We must always think a layer beyond what we see."

Bram wallowed in his role as a phrasemaker while Oliver kept his eyes on the sky.

"Our mind holds many dubious beliefs, beliefs that are false conclusions made from the evidence we see. It is our own flawed attempt to cope with these inconsistencies that lay bare our inferential shortcomings."

The Pimm's finally issued its finishing touches on Bram as his words began to slur together. "And the price we pay for not knowing our own shortcomings is severe. . . *Hiccup* . . . Flawed thinking . . . *Hiccup* . . . is a slippery slope. Because what we think is what we do . . . *Hiccup* . . ."

Bram lifted his right elbow. His hand flopped behind his neck. "You see patterns in the sky. You see order in the world, but it's all just chaos . . . and the mind cannot deal with such a thing."

Bram's head dipped back. His eyes closed, and his hands dropped like branches overweight with squirrels. "But perhaps because we are inept . . . *Hiccup*. That is what makes us human. What we really seek is approval . . . a pat on the back from others . . . recognition . . . a feeling of importance . . . *Snore*."

Bram was burnt toast.

Oliver quietly watched the sky flip in color. When a firework would pop, a wave of happiness rippled through him as he thought about what he had already accomplished on his journey. At midnight, the finale roared.

As Oliver watched the fireworks dissolve into the night, he contemplated the year ahead, wondering if life would only grow more complicated and entangled as he experienced more and more of the disorder in the world. He thought back to the cairn he had seen when he left home. Time is so capable of crumbling the things we build, he wouldn't have been surprised if the cairn had toppled. With the sky now wholly black, he ruminated on how much energy it takes to keep the things we cherish from collapsing. Oliver wondered why he had allowed the most beautiful thing in his life to fall to pieces. Perhaps it was just meant to be that way. Maybe there was an overpowering force he could not see. Or maybe he simply hadn't given enough of his energy to keep love going.

Bram was still slack when Oliver dropped from the table and walked along. Around the next bend he passed a coffee shop. There were a few people inside, sipping and smoking, and celebrating the new year. Oliver took a cup of java and sat against the wall. To his left, a woman with coal-black eyes removed a rolling paper and set it on her table. She filled it with an odorous, green-and-purple plant with shiny crystal fibers, then licked her lips and spun a straight and smooth utensil. She lit the end.

The smoke was viscous and calm. She glanced at Oliver and extended the medicine his way, nodding. Oliver absorbed the pill and he felt it begin to settle him.

Oliver and the woman proceeded until only a thumb's-worth remained. Then she rose, smiled, and exited into the night. Oliver was still as he sipped on his coffee. He felt balanced, and again he remembered that life would guide him and take him where he was meant to be. His mind cleared of angst and his heart grew unburdened. It had been a strange day, but as he sat in solitude, his apprehension melted into an inner peace and a deafening quiet.

And he thought, *At times, silence is all that's needed.*

THE AVIATOR

OLIVER MADE FRIENDS with his hostel manager over the next days. The manager was a woman around thirty with auburn hair and a freckled nose. She spoke with a tranquility that told Oliver she had settled into life and wasn't chasing more.

Approaching the end of his stay, Oliver took to her for advice on where to head next. She spoke of an unusual account that had caught her attention a few months back. A group from London had flown across the English Channel on a hot air balloon. The man who owned the balloon was said to give rides during the weekdays. London to the Nederland in the morning, and the opposite in the evening.

The idea intrigued Oliver. He took her suggestion, and the next afternoon he thanked the manager, and went outside to hail a taxi.

The taxi pulled up to the launch pad tucked behind a metal refinery. The balloon aviator, Albert, stood against the edge of the gondola writing in a small notepad as Oliver walked over. Oliver had to get alarmingly close before Albert looked up with a timid smile that had seen thousands before. His broad, flat nose commanded his face along with wire-rimmed glasses. Behind the black frames were two black eyes, which, judging by the frequency of his blinks, appeared to be dry. Albert assisted Oliver aboard, then tugged one of the four pilot cords harnessed to the sail, and they lifted off. The air that day was a silver, nebulous musk and the balloon was like a floating ruby gleaming in the mist.

As they ascended, Oliver stuck his nose over the basket to view the urban grid from overhead. The complex of canals looked like mine tunnels, cutting through a swampland of weathered-brick tract houses. The city slowly faded as the aircraft climbed and pierced through a layer of fog. Albert pumped the burner and looked out over the expanse.

"The world has become so big, it can be hard to find your way."

Oliver rattled away the usual questions one asks on your first balloon ride—things like how long Albert had been piloting, how long their trip would take, and how much the wind would affect this estimation.

Albert then gave Oliver a tour of the ship. It was basically a lot of helium, a big sheet of nylon, and an oversized basket. Afterward, Oliver asked, "What were you writing about when I walked up?"

Albert was cautious, but he revealed that he was writing a book, and that he had always wanted to be an author.

"That's half the fun of this balloon, Oliver. As I fly people around, I get to use them as characters in my book! I pilot the ship and imagine where my passengers come from and what they're going to do after I drop them off."

"Well, would you like to hear where I've been? That way you don't have to imagine."

"Do we know each other well enough for that?"

Oliver laughed. "Don't you know when you've made a friend?"

Albert rolled his eyebrows like a caterpillar inching along. "It just seems so soon."

"Well, perhaps after I share, we can be friends. Or we can wait until we land. It's up to you how long we wait."

Oliver detailed his journey, its ups and the downs and everything in between. Albert studied the words closely, and at each major turning point, he peeled his face back and wiped the fog from his glasses.

When Oliver finished, Albert moved across the gondola. "You have been through a lot, and yet, you've come to me unscathed. Something powerful is pulling you across the world, Oliver, and I intend to very carefully include you in my book." He stuck out his hand.

"Friends?"

"Friends."

Oliver rerouted their conversation. "Now, since I'm going to be in your book, I think it's fair that I know what it's about."

Albert's reply was not what Oliver expected. He was shy. "It's only a moderately interesting story, Oliver. I still have a lot to work out."

"Well, how many pages have you written?"

"Pages? It's not the number of pages that matters, it's the number of words. And not just the number, it's the quality of the words that counts."

Oliver was amused. How often we think of things one way, only to be enlightened on a better way to think.

"I have 23,256 words, but I don't think I have a single quality one. How am I supposed to piece words into sentences and paragraphs and pages and chapters and have it make sense for a whole book? No, no; it is not ready for another's eyes."

Oliver found himself disappointed in Albert. The aviator hadn't garnered the strength to stick his nose into the alley of literary criticism. He hadn't even begun the journey of rejection and mass revision. *Why is this man so cowardly about something he seems to love?* the boy thought.

Then Oliver considered the upside of Albert's book, of the scholarly enthusiasm and thematic analyses that generation after generation would develop as they read his text. Oliver asked the pilot, "Will you ever at least try to have people read it? So many good things could happen!"

Albert, still coy, said, "But my writing isn't any good, and I'm not sure it ever will be. I've read the masterpieces, and I can't imagine myself producing anything on that level."

"But surely the timeless authors started where you are now! No matter the field you're in, everyone has to work to be great. People who impact society have endured thousands of hours of practice in whatever it is they do. So, if you want to influence the world, you have to work much longer and harder than everyone around you. Albert, don't stop writing and do start believing in yourself, because greatness isn't esoteric or elusive, it just needs to be brought out of you."

Albert's face lit up. He looked at the boy, then gave a tug to one of the chords. "You are quite right. Do you know why people read, Oliver?"

The boy did not.

"People read to escape reality and let the mind wander. It's the same with movies and TV. We're all looking for something, Oliver, and most of the time, we have to turn to places where our minds can be free."

This notion stirred in Oliver for a moment. He then realized the tragedy of Albert's business. Isolation had caused the aviator to lose faith in himself.

Albert withdrew a brass telescope from his coat and scanned the horizon. Staring through the lens, he spoke. "This may sound odd, particularly from someone who spends so much time in the open air, but it is easy to feel like a fish in the sky, like I'm in a glaucous aquarium, like I'm confined in the clouds."

Albert pocketed the instrument, shuffled his hand inside his jacket and removed his notepad. "But even though I sometimes feel lost, as long as I can write, I am well. It is the plasticity of it that does me in."

Albert flipped through to a blank page, then spoke of the notepad. "I keep this handy when a good passage comes to mind. The only salvation for a writer is to write. And when it's good, it comes easy."

Albert pulled out an egg-yolk fountain pen and wrote aloud. His words bled out not only as ink, but in a hyperrealist rendering, what Albert wrote literally came to life in the world around them.

"The sun and wind often argue over who has more power," he said.

And suddenly, the sky over the English Channel shifted from overcast and cloudy into a blithe day. The weather around them went soft, and the wind flag fastened to the basket went limp.

"The wind went first. It wanted to prove its strength. It flexed, and it heaved, and . . ."

The wind picked up, and the pennant flag went horizontal. Heavy gusts swirled around the balloon and rocked the basket with ponderous shocks. Oliver gripped the weaving. His stomach rose in his chest. Albert kept on writing, and with a supersonic force, a thrashing crosswind collided with the mouthpiece of the balloon. The basket flipped sideways, and the force sent Albert tumbling into a metal gas canister, knocking him out cold. The pen and notepad fell onto the wicker, the wind disappeared, and the sun returned, settling the air and guiding the balloon back on course. Land was now in sight.

Oliver checked on the aviator. Albert sat upright against the gas canister as if he were doing very hard thinking, but he was thoroughly unconscious. Oliver looked over the basket. The soil was getting nearer and nearer.

Oliver rose in the gondola and ever-so-carefully he brushed his knuckles along the rungs of the four pilot chords that Albert had been using to steer. He wrapped his fingers around one and turned up to the metal frame inside the sail, studying the mechanism which the chords were fastened to. It didn't look too complex. He raised his shoulders with a deep breath, looked up at the chord like he was looking up a shotgun barrel, and tugged.

The balloon dropped a few feet, but quickly steadied.

Handling each action as gingerly as dynamite, Oliver learned which chord did what; one sent them up, one down, one left, and one right. Now to the rudder. It was like a light switch—on was forward, off was backward.

Oliver pulled the chords like a puppet master. As he lowered the aircraft, hot air spilled into the clouds and he gradually eased their way towards an enormous lawn in a public park. As the balloon drew closer, a crowd began to gather on the ground.

Minutes later, miraculously, Oliver set the ship down on the buttery grass.

Not once did it dawn on Oliver that what the crowd saw was a magnificent airship gracefully coming down for a visit. When the balloon settled, he hurdled the gondola and rushed towards the people for help.

But when he returned with a groundskeeper, Albert was up, circling the balloon as he prepared to lift back off. The groundskeeper chided Oliver for crying wolf. "Sure you're not just seeing things?"

Oliver's voice was hollow. "How did he—"

Oliver hurried over to Albert. Albert's pupils were dilated. The blood had returned to his face. All appeared well as the aviator handed the boy his pack. They said basically what you'd expect them to say, except that Albert told Oliver kiddingly that he had landed in the wrong place. Bottom line, this was an excellent outcome.

Oliver tossed his pack over a shoulder and walked away quite fond of Albert. He just wondered if the aviator should consider writing elsewhere now and then—if he should depart from his life of vicarious stories and uniquely portable magic. *There is value in solitude,* the boy thought, *but true courage comes when you share your dreams with others.*

Oliver then thought about his own courage. He thought about Isabella. *Why did I not defend myself? Why did I not stand up and fight for something I love? Why did I just . . . walk away?*

THE CARICATURIST

AFTER HE LEFT Barcelona, Leo returned to Cantabria feeling defeated. Months passed as he sat in school next to the empty desk where Oliver used to sit. Day by day, regret began to devour Leo. Oliver had never come back, and Leo had never heard from him. Leo found himself continually roaming around their town wondering just what had happened to his friend.

At night, Leo would stare at the pack in the corner of his room with disgust. Guilt consumed him. And one day it became too much for Leo. He lifted his pack from the floor and left home, again.

It was a cold, misty afternoon in London. Leo sat defeated on a damp bench just off the River Thames. In the stream of foot traffic before him, an olive-skinned, russet-haired boy scurried across Leo's line of sight. The vision was quick, but it caused the hairs on his neck to perk up. He rose and hustled though the crowd. Walking in stride with the other boy, Leo turned to the familiar face.

"Oliver?"

His feet stopped. Their eyes met. The boy looking at Leo wasn't the same person. Leo was staring into a face of malice, a face fresh with anger. Both boys stood still. People zipped around them like a rock in a stream. Slowly, the spite washed away from Oliver's face.

"It's good to see you, old friend." They hugged.

The boys walked and walked without plan. Here was a new chapter in life, and they both were willing to let it develop when it would. They talked without break, calm and leisurely, and friendly.

The walking stopped at a food truck under a bridge, and as he stood beside the trolley, Leo could see what was coming from far away.

Over Oliver's shoulder, Leo watched as an elderly man in an oatmeal raincoat shuffled towards them, fully immersed in a bowl of soup. Behind him, two teens were racing down the street on bicycles. There clearly was not enough space for them all to pass.

Dring. Dring. The biker bells rang as the teens came up on the man. But the clam chowder was so good. He was so absorbed in its taste.

Dring. Dring. Dring. Dring.

No response.

Leo moved quickly. The bikes whooshed past as Leo pulled the old man out of the way and he and the oatmeal raincoat toppled backwards. Above them, in slow motion, the chowder floated upward, hovered, then fell back to earth, spattering them both.

Oliver rushed to help them up, catching the stink of the sea floor as he did.

The old man stood, quite perplexed, examining the stringy mess all over Leo and himself. He had a thick walrus mustache and baffled white hair. Suddenly, a lightbulb clicked on in his mind.

"Hmm. Sodium nitrate. No, potassium nitrate. No, maybe trimethoxy benzoic acid. Yes. Yes!" Something extraordinary happened in his face. "I have just the thing. You!" The old man pointed to Leo. "Follow me." And he turned to race off.

Leo exchanged awed eyes with Oliver, then called to the man, pointing at his friend. "What about him?"

Mid-sprint, the oatmeal raincoat dug into his heels and looked back. "Oh, him. Right. He can come too!"

Oliver and Leo followed in a brisk jog to keep up. When they stopped seven blocks later, they were outside a university hall. The boys followed the old man in, anxious as they tried to figure out what would happen next. They went in a door with a sign outside:

Professor Charlie Evans

College of Natural Sciences

Professor Charlie's classroom was more of an auditorium; there were twenty rows of amphitheater seats to their left and a long desk with lab equipment and sinks in front. To the right was a mountainous blackboard and two small doors. One was open, and clearly his office, and the other was shut and read: *Controlled Chemicals.*

The boys set down their packs and looked at the chalkboard, which was the size of a soccer pitch. On the left side were lecture notes, and the rest was covered in integrals, algebra, quantum mechanics, and, oddly, caricatures. Little childlike drawings were scattered throughout the mathematics.

While the boys were taking things in, Professor Charlie had his nose in boxes of chemistry equipment. He pulled a few flasks, then unlocked the closet and returned with two large liters, one labeled gallic acid and the other dimethyl sulfate.

While he measured out the chemicals, Professor Charlie noticed the boys examining a sketch of a dog's face. "It's the exaggeration of doodling that I like. I work on math and physics and chemistry all day, and eventually the equations bore me and my mind runs wild. So, I doodle. And I doodle only exaggeration, things that can never be real in our rigid world."

He glared at a set of integrals. "The reason my sketches are chalked all over the place is because as I crack into theorems and paradoxes, sometimes a little puppy pops into my head. And I care more about the puppy than the numbers, so I stop solving and bring the little pup to life!"

The boys didn't question whether the puppy actually had life. Who were they to decide? But they did want to give his caricatures more life, so they asked, "Can we name them?"

Professor Charlie beamed. "Go ahead! Just be sure to use your imagination as you do."

Oliver and Leo faced the blackboard. They carefully assigned names: Fido, the dog with planet-sized eyes; Snippy, the cat with a pistol in his hand; Lars, the lion rollerblading down the beach; and Zane, the zebra horse lounging in the pool.

Professor Charlie continued mixing chemicals before he perked up and rushed the blackboard. Heavily, he marked up a new explanation to one of his theorems, then stepped back and thought out loud. "Variables. Where would we be without them?"

He wiped his brow with the inner elbow of his lab coat, then grabbed an eraser and swept away the previous iteration of his solution. "I wonder where they all go."

The boys replied together. "Where what goes?"

"The erased. Look here." He had his eraser hinged against the board just above a chalked *equals* sign. He wiped it away. "See. Where did those lines just go?"

He came back from his office with a textbook, poking his nose in, then snapping it shut. "Perhaps that is why the universe is so grand. All the other stuff is out there, and all the non-other stuff is here with us."

He grabbed his chin with chemical risk and muttered, "Perhaps what matters is not where the erased *equals* sign went, but where it came from in the first place."

He walked back over to the blackboard and outlined a caricature of a woman's face. "Where do those lines come from?" He tapped the chalk to the side of his dome, planting white bumps of sediment into the pores at his right eyebrow. "And why do they come from this hand?" He studied the palm with chalk in it. "Unusual, very unusual."

Professor Charlie began amalgamating quantum mechanics on the board. Oliver and Leo watched numbers and letters move through a web of logic.

"Ahh. Boys, watch."

He drew a simple four-by-four matrix. "Imagine the entire blackboard is the universe, and each box in this grid represents one person. Now, each box, each person, is a member of a larger system."

Charlie pointed to Leo. "You. You are this box."

He placed a finger on the bottom left square. "You, as this box, can't see the larger system. You only see and affect what is in your reach—yourself, and the boxes around you. And that is what you must focus on. Yourself, and those around you. If we all make ourselves and those around us better, the larger grid, the larger system, will be better as a whole."

Oliver looked at the squares, at their uniformity and their rigidness. He felt a spark in his stomach, a little ember crackling within. He felt enraged, enraged at the idea of perfection, of concreteness, at a society who wants everybody to fit into a mold. He reddened as he thought of Isabella's stepfather, and how Antonio had wanted him to be a mail-ordered suitor for his daughter.

The little ember in Oliver heaved and roared. This was his first taste of manhood, of a primal instinct to seek retribution for things of the past. This was his first taste of the destructive potential that comes with being an impassioned creature of biology. This was the first time that Oliver began to break from his boyish shell.

Leo had been attentively following along and listening to Professor Charlie, but he had that look of astonishment that said he hadn't understood. Leo politely responded to the analogy, "I see," even though he didn't.

Professor Charlie read Leo's face. "I'm not trying to solve the question of the universe. I'm merely explaining the ease of which every person can help to change it. A nice idea!"

Leo grinned, now understanding. "What about the blackboard?"

"A much tougher question. The blackboard has many names, and each is equally as likely as the next. A paradox, an equation, a guiding hand, a vacuum. That is not for me to know."

"Why?" Oliver and Leo again spoke in unison.

"With some things, it is best to learn to like the idea that you don't know, and probably never will. People who say otherwise have closed themselves off to alternative solutions, and the thoroughly informed person is a dreadful thing."

Professor Charlie studied the small square boxes on the chalkboard. "One thing I might add is to remember how big the universe is. We all get absorbed in our own problems and forget that there is a much grander plan out there that we don't even know about. If everyone cleansed themselves of pettiness, humanity could work as a whole, and accomplish far more than we do now. So, when you find yourself worked up over some mundane argument or trivial concern, take time to look at the stunning expanse of the sky, because it is sobering to see how much you don't know."

Sapphire flames began to surge on the lab desk. Professor Charlie rushed to turn off the gas, then dipped a brush into the mysterious potion and strutted over to the stains on Leo's coat. He moved the bristles along the chowder spill and, like ruby slippers in Oz, it disintegrated into thin air. It was strange how unimportant the stain was by then, but Leo was still appreciative. "Professor Charlie! You're brilliant!"

He hugged the professor, who embraced Leo in a way that said he hadn't been hugged in a long time. "What is brilliance but a few odds and ends?"

As Leo backed off, Professor Charlie continued. "What an accusation that is. Brilliance runs parallel with madness in our world, because most people can't see beyond the realms of their own perception. But I guess it doesn't really matter what anyone thinks. The hands on the clock will turn regardless, and the universe will endure, brilliant or not."

He dabbed the brush on his own shirt. "Enough of me. You boys have spent too much time in my cage of equations. But listen, you two, I am quite jealous. You are young and your blackboards still have a lot of room to be drawn on. Just remember that in real life, there are no erasers." He turned to the board muttering to himself, "Youth, a marvelous thing."

The rest of that sentence floated into the ether as Professor Charlie began sketching with a piece of blue chalk. Oliver realized that Professor Charlie was so gifted, such a divine accident of brainpower, that he probably didn't fully understand himself as a person.

Professor Charlie outlined a caterpillar with a thin nose and a wide grin. Then came a wing on the left, and a symmetrical one on the right. It was a butterfly. Professor Charlie radiated with delight as he added stripes to the wings and the realness of the butterfly became clearer and clearer.

Oliver stared at the sapphire sketch, shaken. He searched for a rational connection in the depths of his mind, and within the innermost valley of the latticework, something fey echoed back.

THE MISCREANT

THE PLATFORM WAS full of commuters when the train sang in from the tunnel and rolled down the track. Like a stampeding herd, the impatient crowd piled in through the car doors and searched for empty seats.

The boys pushed into the metal train to find benches lavishly upholstered and every other car lined with private cabins. They were making their way through when Oliver saw a long, thick nest of hair with a deep-blue flower set over the ear. He slowed in the aisle, and edged forward.

"Oliver, hurry up, you maniac!" Leo had the trolley door open and was very concerned about getting a good seat. Oliver moved past the girl, and glanced back just in time for a clear sight. It wasn't Isabella.

Leo was growing anxious. It was their second car and they hadn't found their seats. They were evaluating options when a slim-shouldered man exited a cabin a few yards down. Leo sprinted and slipped in. Oliver followed to find the cabin vacant.

The train wheels began their rotation as the boys set their packs down and leaned their elbows on the foldout table to watch the beehive of commuters swarm about the platform.

The train was in the eighth notch and must've been about midway along in the trip when their cabin door opened. It would be difficult to describe the man who entered. He was a salad of racial genes, medium height, medium build, with no visible scars or markings, and wearing a nondescript black coat, a white Oxford shirt, and black military boots.

The stranger didn't acknowledge the boys as he sat. He placed his black bag by his hips and flapped open a newspaper. On the front column, in thick-bodied black lettering, the headline read, *"New York investment wizard, Anthony Moses, continues expanding his empire in the UK."* Cached below was a photo of that same man from the magazine, with vulpine good looks, crystal-white eyes, and a chin which made him look invincible. Oliver tried to read the article underneath, but when the strange man noticed Oliver looking at him, he folded the paper up and placed it over his bag.

Then he just sat there with wide eyes, stiller than a stone wall, not blinking, looking at a panel of wood above the boys' heads. For a long minute, the scaly texture of an awkward silence lingered in the cabin. Then, without word, the miscreant removed a small, pewter chess set from his briefcase. He placed it on the table and used his skeletal fingers to arrange the board so that each edge paralleled the edge of the table and there was precise proportion in those distances. His tongue slithered out of his mouth as he asked, "We only know as much as our mind can work out, don't you think?"

Oliver shivered at the strange idea.

Neither boy was in the mood for chess, but the miscreant just stared at the board with his head cocked. It was unnervingly obvious that one of them needed to play his game, so Oliver slid along the bench.

When the pawns were up-board, the miscreant gripped the knight and leapt it two checks north and one check west. He had alarming fixation with the leap, like the asymmetry of the knight's movement aroused him. Oliver countered with his white bishop and took the enemy knight. The miscreant looked at Oliver, unhappy to see an opponent who knew what he was doing.

As the game went on, Oliver studied the miscreant in detail—the way he flinched when a passenger walked by the window, the way he wore his clothes with disdain, the way he nervously rubbed his hands across his neck, the way he would not let his briefcase leave his touch. The miscreant's mannerisms left Oliver optimistic that he would soon reveal his agenda.

As the match progressed, the three commuters in the cabin quietly focused on chess.

"You appear to be in an unwinnable position, sir," Leo chimed in as Oliver slid a white pawn up and announced, "Check."

The miscreant let out a cackle and glanced at Leo from the corner of his eyes. The train conductor's voice then broke in over the intercom to announce that they were nearing their Dublin arrival. The miscreant stared at the speakerbox with huge paranoid eyes, turning white and sweaty with the news. *He's definitely not a tourist,* Oliver thought. *I wonder where he's going?*

Oliver pretended to stretch his triceps while putting his voice high and small. "So, what's in Dublin for you?"

The miscreant's bony face twitched across the cabin and looked at his. His cheeks were taut as he searched Oliver's eyes, looking for a reason to trust the boy. There was none. Oliver was probably wearing a wire beneath his shirt. The miscreant hissed, "I'm really not sure."

He loosened his collar as he sacrificed a rook. The miscreant was now an acrobat spanning the tightrope, meticulously observing each inch ahead of him. This read gave Oliver all he needed to win.

Leo probed, "How do you not know what's in Dublin? There must be a reason you're on this train."

The cabin turned cold and quiet like a dreadful, silent ballet. Oliver kicked Leo beneath the table to tell him not to pry any further, and Leo began to regret his question.

The miscreant swallowed his venom and reflected. Perhaps he thought about what he would do in Dublin, or his next chess play, or if he had already said too much. Or maybe about why he was really here—how his shady accounting scam had swindled millions of dollars from mom-and-pop businesses.

Finally, he spoke. "But I'm not here." He glanced at his watch. "I'm on a plane to Istanbul."

The boys exchanged a nervous look. Leo took a big gulp of saliva. "How can you be two places at once?"

"Let's just say that people will be expecting me in Turkey, but it serves me best to head in the opposite direction."

Oliver remained quiet. Leo continued, "And what's waiting in Istanbul?"

The miscreant flashed his sharp teeth as his lips parted into a devilish smile. "Handcuffs."

Oliver became defensive. "For what?"

The miscreant sidestepped the question and blabbered elusively without even appearing to believe what he was saying. His message meant nothing to him; it was a practiced anecdote of lies, and the boys could tell they were dealing with a recent member of society, a masked man with the stench of corruption.

"By the way, I'm Leo. This is Oliver." Leo tried to brighten the mood by sticking his hand out, even though he knew the shake would not be usual by any means. Oliver nodded, fidgeted, then looked at the board, trying to figure out how to get out of the cabin.

"Nice to meet you both." The miscreant spoke off-key and didn't bother to give his name. He reached his hand across the table and shook Leo's with an icy palm.

The players approached the end of the game when the train began decelerating. The miscreant retreated his bishop to protect his king. And when his fingertips left the piece, Oliver could see his slithery face darken, like he was suddenly overwhelmed by a feeling that is common in chess, a disturbing sense that you have just done exactly what your opponent wanted. The miscreant's internal alarm pierced his eardrums as red sweat began accumulating at his hairline. The boy could collect his queen.

Oliver noticed too, but demurred for a minute to analyze the board. It was a clean shot. He thrust over her majesty and declared, "Mate." He had won in only twenty-two moves.

The locomotive settled into its berth and came to a stop. The boys grabbed their packs and stood. No need to say goodbye. They didn't know exactly what the miscreant had done, but they knew he had done something.

With disgust at having lost the game, the miscreant slammed his fists on the foldout table, and when he peered up, the boys were exiting the cabin. Now that they were leaving, he wanted to think of a way to make them stay. He sat with his clenched fists on each side of the chessboard and watched them go. How badly he wanted to call to them and spill his soul, to confess, to someone, anyone, even if it was to these two boys without the slightest idea of the laundry list of felonies he had committed. He was writhing inside. The vile poison of guilt was gushing out of his ears. *Confess! Confess!*

But he couldn't. He just sat there. Cold, and alone.

Oliver and Leo stepped onto the platform and zigzagged their way through a new hive of commuters buzzing about the dead, immobile air.

Minutes later, the miscreant wriggled out of the train.

He wormed his way to a newsstand and scanned the spider web of prints. His face wasn't on any of the covers—and this disappointed him.

The miscreant was experiencing the reality that despite all that is going on in your own life, the world goes on about its business. His story was not a ticket-selling, box-office attraction; it was a draft crumpled up by a screenwriter and lobbed into the trash.

The owner of the newsstand was a calm woman with hazel eyes. She leaned forward on her backless stool and watched the miscreant deviously search her shelves. Observing his angst, she tried to help. Her words came out calmly.

"Sir, do you need anything?"

The miscreant looked at her pleadingly. He needed support, but he was scared. Then his defensiveness kicked in and he saw her as a government agent. Her eyes were digging into his, her face looking for his concealed answers. The miscreant flashed that devious smile and put his finger to his lips. His secret would remain with him forever. He turned, blended into the crowd like a snake in the forest, and disappeared.

His silver bullet would not be far behind.

THE SHEPHERD

THE CLOCK RADIO clicked on at 7:15 AM. Oliver and Leo grabbed their packs and headed out.

The boys had planned to visit a museum, but the line outside was packed, so they moved on.

It felt great outside. The boys were strolling along a large park when Oliver noticed a trail of ants at his feet. Someone had dropped half a banana on the sidewalk, and these little creatures were farming the fruit to return to their pantries. Oliver decided to follow the trail. The single-file row crossed obstacles and scaled debris as they passaged home, and when Oliver saw their hill, he paused and thought about how one gust of wind, one sheet of rain, or one whip from a lawn mower could start an avalanche and destroy all that the colony had built. But now, the hill stood strong. It didn't matter how long or rocky their road had been; what mattered was that they were in it together, and together, they had made it home.

Oliver rose from the hill and found himself at the head of the lawn. He stood and listened to the quiet that comes in the early morning, until the he heard a laugh coming from the pitch. Frolicking around the lawn was a magnificent beast with a pale face, brown ears, and a black neck. The shepherd dog ran along the grass, looping in circles and chasing different scents.

Leo came over with his water bottle and instructed Oliver to scoop his hands into a bowl-shape. Oliver felt the water drip through the cracks of his fingers as he knelt and whistled the shepherd over.

Her brown ears straightened before she galloped across the lawn and dipped her head for refreshment. As the water bowl emptied, a man ran onto the lawn holding an empty leash. He was panting as he removed his khaki Homburg and rubbed the back of his neck, staring at the pooch as if he had been chasing her for weeks. "Mavi! Mavi! Thank you for finding her."

Oliver and Leo laughed. "We just offered her water and she came right over."

The keeper smiled at the shepherd as he began to perspire. "I've been running all over. She ran across the street and I lost her . . . should've checked the lawn first. She's always been a runner."

This man had wavy blonde hair, a prognathous jaw, and prominent eyes. His appearance suggested that of a cultured fellow, maybe someone who had been bred into aristocracy but never found a way to escape it altogether. Maybe he was like many young men who thought having a degree from a decent school automatically rewarded him with vast riches. Maybe it was this reality which flustered him so much.

His pearly white teeth stuck a smidgeon over his lip when he said, "Well! You saved me, boys. Mavi means everything to her owner." He linked the leash to the shepherd's gold collar. "Come, come, Mavi. Let us introduce your rescuers to Mr. Moses."

He motioned for the boys to follow, then turned with a brisk walk. The boys shrugged at each other and followed.

When they reached the perimeter of the park, Mavi began to race ahead. Twelve long leaps took her and her keeper into a charming little tobacco boutique. The boys shuffled in after them.

The tobacco house harkened back to the era when smoking was king, and all business was conducted over an ashtray. It was full of dark work, friendly counters, and a lingering haze of crop. That was the first thing that the boys noticed—the delicious smell of aged tobacco.

The shop had no occupants except for two gentlemen across the room. Mr. Moses, Mavi's owner, was in a tweed sports coat and leather riding boots. One would not call him tall or heavy, but his presence radiated an unchallengeable aura. He resembled a noble conqueror who ruled with an iron fist in a velvet glove, a man who had no intention of placing his fate with anyone other than himself.

Moses stood on the other side of a display case from the shop's owner, who had a warm hatchet face and was dressed in a crimson quarter-zip pullover and a plaid Jaxon hat. Both these men held ivory Meerschaum pipes in their hands.

Moses, seeing Mavi, set his pipe on a padded sheath, then knelt to scratch behind her ears. Oliver now noticed his face. Moses had vulpine good looks, crystal-white eyes, and a chin of invincibility. He was the man from the magazine and the paper. Some sort of overlord from America who was buying up assets left and right. Oliver was sure of it, but he kept quiet.

Moses tried the keeper. "All is well, I trust?" There was a soft undercurrent of tension, as if he was astounded that everything seemed to be alright.

The keeper brushed past the incident with a steel voice. "Mavi made some friends."

Moses studied the boys and thanked them for playing with Mavi, who was wagging her tail with joy. Moses trusted her judgment more than anyone, and whatever doubt he may have had about these boys was trumped by her approval. He then motioned to the keeper, who straightened and drifted out into the street.

Moses addressed Oliver and Leo. "Familiar with this part of the world?"

Shrugs.

"Ever been to a horse track?"

Same result.

"Up to watch a few races with me?"

The boys nodded.

Moses escorted Mavi and the boys out to a regal black limousine. The keeper reached through the window and handed Mavi her bone. Moses thanked him, hit the window up, and snatched the bone from Mavi's jaw. He tossed it to the other end of the limo bay. "It's the repetition she loves. As much as each run is similar, none of them are the same."

On the ride to the track, they occasionally played Mavi's game, but mostly just idled in a symphony of traffic. The boys guessed Moses would be irritated at the lines of cars, but he spoke of the delay with an even keel. He had Mavi's bone in his hand while looking out the window.

"Things never happen the way you want. Diversions come every day, and they come objectively. It's always your decision how these inconveniences weigh on you . . . and complaining never lightens the load."

Their excitement grew when they arrived. The horse track was nearly the size of a stadium. Cars were parked along dozens of rows and a long entry line of people curved around the gate. Moses' caravan rolled to the front and entered through a private gate.

He winked at the boys over his shoulder. "I just bought this place. We've got great seats."

"Nothing is won on the first turn. If there's one thing jockeys should know, it's when to slow down." The next set of horses were led to the starting gate.

And sure enough, halfway in, the highbred out front toppled over in a geyser of muddy sand. "See, boys, discipline and intelligence win the race, not the heaviest foot."

They enjoyed the races from a suite with three rows of seats, bar food, drinks, and cigars. By the second race, the foxhole was roaring as everyone began drinking and smoking their ears off and babbling about the conditions of the track and betting strategies. Moses, Mavi, and the boys had the front seats. Moses removed a gold lighter and gold cutters from his sports coat, then snipped the end of his stick. The lighter's shiny jaws snapped shut, and he drew his first wreath. He pointed to a black thoroughbred proudly modeling in the winner's circle.

"That horse'll never make it to the big leagues."

Oliver asked, "How do you know, sir?"

"It's not because the horse isn't capable. He's a powerful specimen. It's not because he isn't capable. That horse is a powerful specimen. It's not because of the jockey either. The problem is the owner. The owner takes too much pleasure seeing his prized stallion win. He enters him in these easy races for the ceremonial ribbon, not for the betterment of the horse. And you know what happens? The stallion never gets any faster. And why should he? He runs how he runs and he always wins.

"The only way that horse'll start to post better times is if the owner puts him in a competitive race. Of course, the horse would probably lose at first, but his time would be faster. The horses around him—more trained and more experienced—would push him, and in the long run, he'd be better because of it. It's a shame to waste such talent." His cheeks narrowed as he pulled in another drag, and he smiled as smoke drifted across his teeth. "Maybe I'll buy him."

As the afternoon burned on, Moses grew blunter, reminiscing on his early days.

"My mother was a humble, hard-working woman. She raised me herself. A blue-collar job by day, and a parent by night. One evening, she says to me, 'I work my life away doing things I don't want to, all for you. And eventually, you will do have to do things you don't want to, all for me and your future family. That's just life.' I patiently listened to my mother, but what she didn't realize was that I already was doing things I didn't like. I didn't like listening to adults who hadn't accomplished much. I hated our pygmy lifestyle. I hated feeling guilty that she had to do things she didn't like, for me. It was then and there that I packed up, left her a note, and took off. I wanted to do things for her, things for my future family, that I loved. It may sound ironic, but I knew I had to go far from home to make that happen.

"I knew I had to get out of my bubble. I knew it because while everyone around me was distracted by the outcome of a football game or the weight of some insecure actress, people kept telling me that I worked too hard and that I needed to relax a bit. I couldn't disagree more. Relaxing is for after you've accomplished something, after you've added value to the world. I knew I needed to go because I saw how everyone was sucked into a myth, glued to their televisions, stapled to the headlines . . . sheep who are told what to do, who to hate, who to love, how to live. I just didn't want my life to be like that, so I insulated myself from the culture I once cherished. And I knew no one would understand. I knew no one could see that there was something innate driving me, something thicker than opinion, and I knew that not even my own mother could see that I was different.

"So, I said screw it. Screw what they think. Because I knew it didn't matter. I knew myself, and I knew what I needed to do. So I left everything and everyone, and I went across the world and didn't look back. I wanted to see it all. I wanted to see who was happy and why they were that way. I just kept thinking that I didn't want to say the same things at eighty that I had at twenty. And now, even with everything I've done, I value those early years the most. Plus, my mother doesn't have to do stuff she doesn't like anymore."

Moses took a long draw of tobacco, then waved his hand to everyone in the suite, instructing everyone to clear out. Everyone zippered their teeth and left in a fast fade. The suite was an empty canyon of smoke. Moses exhaled and rotated towards the boys.

"A man's disposition is shown by many things, but certainly by the way he handles his smoke. The anxious man taps his finger to the wrapper to force the ash; the tranquil man lets it be. The anxious rip through the smoke and never allow it to breathe; the tranquil nurture it but never let it fade."

Moses set his stick on the table. "I've noticed that you each relish your flame. You each avoid premature action. And that is rare, especially at your age. It tells me that you are neither senselessly frightened nor recklessly optimistic. These are intangibles I value, and they are very hard to teach."

The boys sensed that something else was on the table here.

"Funny thing. I see myself in you boys. I see your confidence and ambition. I see that you possess many irreplaceable assets."

He took another draw. "It is through the influence of certain individuals that the development of our world is directed. And it is the duty of the current guard to source the next set of leaders." Moses rubbed Mavi's back. "Would you two consider coming to work for me? I'm very interested to see who you might grow up to be. Besides, how long can you really keep up this adventure?"

Mavi thumped her tail against the floor in approval. Moses and the boys spoke of terms, of duties, of life in America while their sticks burned. When an agreement was reached, they laid their sticks across the ashtray and let them fade out naturally.

The following morning, Moses and Mavi scooped up the boys on the way to the airport. They drove past security, up on the tarmac, and parked next to a leviathan of an airliner. Their chauffer, with his grey suit, solid black tie, cap, and gloves, handed their luggage directly to the airline mechanic. Moses took note of the boys' minimalism in their packs, and spoke over the idling engines.

"Light travelers. I like it. You two sure are going to start fresh!"

The stewardess escorted them to the first-class section of the transatlantic flight. Oliver nestled himself in the window seat, and as they began their taxi, he spotted something out the corner of his eye, something hovering over the metal wing.

He shook his head and looked again. There was no evidence that the mirage existed, but from his seat, Oliver thought it looked like a butterfly. It fluttered hither and thither, inking substance into his head. His vision was clear and bright and even a rip sharper than usual, but as he tried to focus, the impression of the phantom overlapped on itself.

He tapped Leo and pointed out towards the wing. But when he turned back, only sunlight reflected off the aluminum spoiler. The butterfly was a dissident renegade stalking the boy. Oliver closed his eyes and willed himself to think of nothing; he had to avoid losing his grip. But he could neither confirm nor deny what he had just seen.

The turbines churned faster and faster, and the airplane began to climb over the clouds.

The sun always sets in the west.

THE PIANIST

THE PIANIST RIPPLED soothing notes beside the crystal staircase. He had always admired the nouvelle atmosphere of the Bel Étage. Set over his shoulders was a white dinner jacket with a long tailcoat, and beneath his jaw was a black satin bowtie.

The pianist was a wizard with the keys. He sat with a stiff posture and tapped the foot pedals as his hands alternated along the white-and-black board, integrating sharp bagatelle plots into the broader range of his one-man symphony. The pianist was a supreme brain, and anyone who had the pleasure of speaking with him could see the calculus of electromagnetic activity behind his eyes. So, for the pianist, this soft morceau was nearly subconscious.

The beveled glass stairwell next to him rose like a three-cornered ruler with a quarter turn in the middle. If you stood beside the pianist, climbed the first flight of steps, turned left, rose the second flight, and followed this path once more, you'd find yourself well above the dining room. Oliver was up on this level, standing in a seven-fold tie and virile suit, looking out into the Bel Étage when he met H.B.

"Sir, your water . . . please!" H.B. called up to Oliver. He was sprawled out on the elegant stairwell in filth-green clothes, with dirt on his face, and stinking like a dumpster. He looked drunk, like the kind who woke up on the bottle and only let go of it once he fell asleep. Oliver could never truly learn how H.B. fell that low, because even if the drifter wanted to tell, this was a man who lived to forget.

Oliver couldn't ignore this sight. H.B. was a blight in this domain of chandeliers, epicureanism, and general excellence. *How did such a lowlife get in?* Oliver grimaced; his mind flooded with impurities.

"Sir, please! Water," H.B. pleaded again. Oliver checked his hands for a bottle, but they were empty. *What is this brainchild looking at?* Oliver turned up the flight of steps to see the horologist descending from the unmarked door. He was well-coiffed and baronial in his tux.

The horologist held a murky bottle of half water and half mud as he walked down and greeted Oliver, stretching out his hand. "This is all I have, Oliver. Here you go."

Before accepting the bottle, Oliver looked at the contaminants floating in the water, then turned on the landing and scanned the fine restaurant. On each table were glasses of clean water. A young, male attendant carried a fresh pitcher around for refills. This didn't make sense. He began to descend the bevel staircase. Surely the kitchen could spare a glass. Oliver led himself down the diaphanous levels. He took a tight turn to the right and continued down the next flight. Then he repeated this same action, and froze. Oliver was now above the horologist and H.B.

The horologist glanced up. "Some boundaries seem like they'll go on forever. You can keep fighting and fighting them, but you'll never get to where you're going. Sometimes, you must reassess the boundary itself to see that most limitations, like fears, are just an illusion. Only when we have exposed such a fabrication are we able to step outside the loop."

It was clear that the horologist wanted Oliver to learn something in this moment. He stepped down and took the plastic bottle. His grip compressed the thin container and sent a cloud of suspended solids up into the water.

Why is this the only option? Oliver thought. He studied the mixture swirling in his hand, then realized, *Who am I to clear the muddy water?* He grew patient, and the water cleansed itself from the mud as the heavy silt drifted to the bottom. *There are forces much larger than ourselves,* he thought. *At times, there is great advantage in inaction.*

Oliver carefully descended the stairs to H.B. and handed him the water, cautioning him to sip from the top with care. Then Oliver and the horologist began to climb to the unmarked door. Out of earshot, Oliver asked, "Why give him anything? Doesn't that just encourage his behavior?"

The horologist calmly shook his head. "Oliver. Oliver. That poor soul usually only speaks to himself. H.B. must have seen some good in you."

"Good in me? He must be mad."

The horologist grinned. "Things aren't always as they seem. You may only pass by that fellow once. It's best to do any good you can while you have the chance." Now at the portal, the horologist placed his hand on Oliver's shoulder. "I'd like to show you something."

The door was a shade below black and had a white, parallelogram handle with no keyhole. The realm which they stepped into had no height. No length. No dimension. It was a place without simple answers or explanations.

In front of them was a clock of cosmic proportion. It was a derivation of something infinite, a substrate of a supreme fabric. The satellite-sized dial was lathered white, with platinum bearings and bold markings. Behind the dial swayed a titanic pendulum, which swung back and forth in asymmetrical shifts. Between the men and the dial, hovering over the black-and-white tiled floor, were two mechanical gears. One black, one white. The simplicity of these instruments suggested extreme complexity.

The horologist spoke with solace. "I caution you to prepare yourself, Oliver." He moved to the hovering mechanics. "This black gear, Oliver, is death. It slows down time when a soul passes."

Turning to its white brother, "And this is life; it speeds up time to balance death. The white gear propels time forward, and the black gear pushes time backward. Time is based on their resonance."

Oliver watched as the gears opposed each other with countering clicks. "Each time death backs up, life must work harder. Oliver, I'm concerned that one day the white gear will fail. Aeon upon aeon have flowed through these gears, and at some point, one must give."

Somewhere behind the bliss, bewildered shadows conferred. Oliver sensed the gravity of these statements. "What can I do to help?"

"Unfortunately, Oliver, it is not up to me." The horologist handed him a pair of unnumbered die—one white, the other black. "Remember, Oliver, death is only a change in time."

Oliver looked up from his hand as the horologist slipped back out the door. Oliver followed, but when the white knob flipped shut, the door morphed into the black-and-white checkered tile that was around the room. Oliver understood that he was meant to stay, and that the horologist again wanted him to learn something.

He made way back to the oscillating gears, now grasping what he had been asked to do. He expanded his chest, tightened his forearm, and tossed the contrasting die across the floor. They rolled and toppled and rolled and toppled. The echoes ricocheted off the tile with increasing sound as the die trundled near the swaying pendulum. And when they crossed its path, the erratic metronome swung itself and knocked them into a further cascade. And something changed.

The black and white die began snowballing in size as they absorbed the tiles. Each flip of their faces absorbed more and more matter as the die grew into behemoth cubes.

The black die had just recoiled off a wall and was headed directly towards the white gear of life when the horologist's words came back to him. *Only when we have exposed fabrication are we able to step outside the loop.* Oliver planted his feet in front of the white gear as blackness toppled towards him. The towering die seethed with faint internal shadows and snapped down on Oliver like the hammer of a .357 Magnum. Oliver was nothing in that moment. It was not as simple as darkness or an absence of light. It was just silent. Oliver was compressed to the point where he could be no more.

Suddenly, he was back atop the bevel staircase above the restaurant. He felt irreducible and inviolate, vast and incalculable. Neither H.B. nor the horologist was there. The only person on the steps was a handsome bathroom attendant. Oliver turned back towards the unmarked door. It read, *Men's*. A restroom. Oliver headed for the bar, just looking to escape this macrocosm.

He strolled past the pianist to get a drink, and finished it leaning against the piano, not sure if was dreaming or awake. A hand came to his shoulder followed by a soft voice. "Oliver?"

He turned, and what he saw frightened him.

She was radiant and glowing, a model with gorgeous cheekbones sharp enough to carve ice. It was Isabella, wearing a white cocktail dress and looking like heaven. Oliver could not take his eyes away. In this land of tropes and misdirection, Isabella had come back to him.

Oliver shifted towards her, and she to him. Her breasts rested against his chest as Oliver set his palm to her cheek. Their eyes closed. Their lips met. It was everything they had been waiting for. Everything.

But when Oliver opened his eyes, Isabella was disappearing into starlight, and she held the heavy alloy pocket watch Oliver had seen before. She turned his hand and set it in his palm. Oliver was inanimate as he watched her fade. The pianist stopped playing and looked at Oliver's solemn face. "Love is not what you have, Oliver. Love is what's left over, after time has burned everything away."

Oliver stared blankly, his hand out as Isabella's palm dissolved over his.

The pianist resumed. His hands navigated the board while he spoke, looking at Oliver.

"We spend our lives waiting until we're perfect or bulletproof to go after what we really want. Don't squander opportunities that may not be recoverable. Don't turn your back on the things that truly matter in your heart. Time only speeds up as you go. Don't wait to do what's right."

Oliver could sense that, in this complex multiverse, a far-reaching and illimitable plan was being devised. But there was still that one lingering question. It had yet to be addressed and might never be a concern, but the question was still there.

THE MENTOR

THE SAME RESTLESS energy that inspired Oliver and Leo to leave home had propelled them across hemispheres all the way to New York City. Moses signed them to his investment firm and mentored them for five years in the lucrative business of real estate private equity. During the first year, his staff put Oliver and Leo through a rigorous analyst program. The following four were spent directly shadowing their mentor.

As the boys grew into young men, they gained impressive insight from Moses. With each year of prosperity, the comfort of success settled further and further in, and with each year of experience, Oliver and Leo grew busier and busier with their work. Time accelerated, but not forward. It expanded geometrically in a flat disk, spiraling outward from its epicenter. For Oliver and Leo, life had grown quickly, then tapered out. Everything they had done, they seemed to do over and over again. Days were indistinguishable, superimposed from office to office, subway to subway, nightclub to nightclub, restaurant to restaurant. A VHS tape on fast-forward, zipping along.

It was early morning with the sun not shining in New York City. Leo had finished his breakfast and was reading the Saturday paper while Oliver was still eating. Leo took notice, but didn't say anything as he watched Oliver comb through a letter he received in the mail.

Once Oliver had settled in financially, he'd hired a private investigator to try and get back in touch with Isabella. Part of it was curiosity, part of it was just having the means, but deep down there was a small ember of hope that burned in the young man.

Unfortunately, Isabella had left for university while Oliver was with Gabriel the clothier. Isabella's parents declined to provide information about their daughter's whereabouts. The private eye had informed Oliver that no university would supply confidential information about their students, and that because he never received a lead, he had no way of knowing where to look, or where Isabella might have gone after that. Yet, twice a year, the investigator would still send a letter confirming the status of the case. Leo recognized the look of distress on Oliver's face, and tried to turn his attention to something else.

"Got to leave in fifteen. All set for these meetings?"

Oliver dropped the letter beside his plate, nodded, and took the coffee to his room to shower.

Oliver and Leo were in Grand Army Plaza two hours later. Moses held a folded newspaper under his arm and jawed to another man on the curb. "I'm only interested in the exceptionally rare at this point." The men shook hands, turned back-to-back and proceeded in opposite directions, each with an entourage at their hip. That concluded the first meeting.

From twenty paces away, Moses looked like a mountain of health. He was six foot one with heroic shoulders and a butch walk. Close-up, though, his face was leaden. Above his creased forehead were thinning locks of white hair. No matter—Moses was still a brilliant investment tactician of imposing power. He was still methodical, and majestic.

Oliver, in his windowpanes, and Leo, in his pinstripes, strutted by his side. They had become the very model of industrious and enterprising young men. They were seriously handsome, but their success came with a color that gave their faces weight beyond their years.

The cadre's next stop was an executive conference room on the forty-fourth floor of a skyscraper. Moses and his team stood before the office building on this weekend morning with sincere distaste. There were mortgages to be paid, cars to be purchased, and private school tuitions to be billed. Money had its flexed grip around their necks; it had them working on their day off.

The squadron of lawyers, accountants, and the investment team marched into the high-ceilinged, marble lobby and made for the elevators.

"Closed."

This word was an earthquake. The gentleman seated behind the reception desk notified them that the elevators were down. Moses froze and began a short spasm of coughing. "What?" His voice echoed across the white tundra of the lobby.

The third in the annual wave of snowstorms had knocked out the power to the elevators. Moses and his team were now forced to climb forty-four flights up to the meeting. The lumpy businessmen wheezed and barked as they lugged their briefcases and bellies up the frigid concrete steps. Their team had pored over all the little details of the negotiation so they could enter the meeting with unencumbered minds; but now, that objective was shot.

In the conference room, the cold and sweaty group dropped their coats and took seats around the executive table. Everyone sat but Moses, who stood before the floor-to-ceiling window and looked out north over the skyline. If Central Park is where fortunes are spent, this was where they were made. The view was worth a million bucks. He studied it and imagined the Upper East and West sides wrapping the park like a diamond necklace.

Eighty minutes later, at the tail-end of the meeting, every glass of mineral water was empty. The contract had been executed and the legal counsel now robotically congratulated the counterparty, "Gentlemen, you are now the owner of 6 Bond Street."

As everyone began packing their supplies, a taunt echoed off the table. "Moses, thanks for the cherry."

This transparent provocation came from the new owner of 6 Bond Street. He had an oily voice and wore droopy eyes, a doctored face, and slicked-back hair, which resulted in a forehead that could only be described as a sniper's dream. If that wasn't enough, his frumpish suit was a measurement too wide and it had a gaudy, double-tiered lapel that should have remained in the nineteenth century.

No one had moved, and no one had said a word, when Leo, wanting to defend Moses, straightened his spine to speak words that would end in false teeth. But Moses sternly indicated that nothing was to be said. Leo's mannerisms reverted in his chair.

The purchasing team then exited, and every pair of eyes faced Moses. All decisions passed directly from his hand, and there was never a breakdown in discipline. Oliver and Leo remembered their mentor's creed from early on. "In fighting, you never get enough, but in yielding, you get more than expected." And they had seen how this worked for Moses. He was notoriously straitlaced and had an improbable success rate on deals with infinitesimal odds. Moses never became angry. He never made a threat. Moses was a man of principle.

"Not everyone is bound by civil conventions. Let's all forget about it. Besides, he overpaid."

The conference room slowly cleared as the team sectioned off to their individual offices. Oliver and Leo stayed behind. Moses, still standing before the window, sighed. On the wall opposite the window hung a colossal painting of a lion. The beast had been fabulously depicted in a rich golden hue, which made him look intentionally elegant.

"You know, every time I look over my shoulder in these meetings, my eye catches that painting. Do you know what it reminds me of?"

Oliver and Leo took a moment to observe the canvas and its mass applicability. Their mentor went along.

"Every morning in the safari, both the lion and the gazelle wake. If the gazelle is going to survive, it must outrun the slowest member of its pack. It doesn't matter where they are headed; it doesn't matter how the gazelle feels that day. The gazelle has to run. The lion is defined by the same rules. No matter where the pack of gazelle is headed, no matter how the lion feels, no matter what it wants, the lion must get to running. Every living creature in this world has to wake up and run to survive. That's what the mural represents—a reminder to stay on the hunt."

Leo flipped his foot over his thigh and faced the picture more directly. "And how do you tell a lion from a gazelle?"

Moses took a chair across the empty table. "The gazelle is only running because the lion is chasing him. If the lion were to stop, the gazelle would stop. But a lion wakes and runs because he loves the hunt. People think a lion is who he is because of how ferocious he is when he chases his prey. But what they don't think about, what truly defines the king of the jungle, is that when a lion sees a wounded gazelle, he sits quiet, and lets the wounded pass."

"Why is that?" Oliver asked.

"Because eating is not a concern for him. That will happen one way or another. The challenge that the lion lives for is outmaneuvering the capable, healthy, and able gazelle. That is what drives his paw." Moses fidgeted in his chair. "Oliver. Leo. When we met years ago, I saw the lion in two cubs. I saw your potential, and the magnetism and animal force you both carried. You've hunted with me for a long time and have grown so much. But when we met, you were hungry, off on an adventure, on the prowl. I fear that you have grown comfortable and complacent. And I cannot be the lion who tames his cubs. It's time you two return to the frontier and relearn the hunt. I have domesticated my beasts, and I will not do so anymore. Come."

The boys wearily followed Moses down the icy stairwell and back outside where vinegary steam purled and twisted from the cavities of the streets. When they reached a white-and-black building on the southern border of the park, Moses sunk his heels into the concrete.

"No matter how smart you think you are, you have to have a place to start. You two now have an exceptionally strong foundation, and you must now build yourselves up."

Moses looked to the top of the skyscraper. "Remember, it takes years to rise, but less than a minute to fall. Never gloat; never let outrageous pride or arrogance soil your thought; never dismiss rationality because you think you have it all figured out. Or you will slip."

They continued their walk, passing a lot of people. The ones who stood out were not the traveling tourists who loitered on the sidewalk with a camera around their neck and sparklers for eyes, with no idea which way was up and which was west. No, the people who stood out were the nearby residents. The people who didn't care what they wore as long as it was Valentino or Dior or Kiton, who didn't care where they ate as long as it was Marea or Cipriani's or Jean-George's, who didn't care where they summered as long as it was Montauk or Monaco or the Maldives. The people who danced in their nests of nobility, and nowhere else.

Halfway between Columbus Circle and the Plaza, the three turned downtown. Oliver's eyes landed on a woman heading straight for them. She moved rapidly in her glossy-black, impractical stilettos, and her locks of blond hair popped with each heel click to the concrete. A red cashmere coat lay open for onlookers to see her jewel-neck dress and cleavage sitting beneath the silk scarf around her throat. This outfit was selected by a designer at Barney's who knew her husband's bank account could routinely take blows of Armani, Saint Laurent, and Christian Louboutin. The cost of her never-on-sale garments would clothe a small village in Africa, but that wasn't her problem. She moved to promote maximum envy from males of status and maximum resentment from everyone else.

As the distance between Oliver and this vixen narrowed, his mind very quickly drifted into the clouds. He offered her his arm and fell in her stride. Oh, may I escort you on your walk home, miss? Are you in the mood for a pre-noon cocktail at the Four Seasons? Oh, you are; perfect, I have nowhere to be. They would each have two martinis and be so lustful that they'd order a third but leave $150 on the table without touching the final round. She probably had a condo stashed somewhere in the Upper East, and they'd have a great afternoon frolicking around her imported, silk sheets.

Oliver returned from the clouds to find that he had been staring at this deity too long. She was looking right at him, and she enjoyed his attention. She stared right back with a provocative look—a confident, vogue gaze which acknowledged her own libidinous desires. A look that said she had shared Oliver's daydream. A look that also said Oliver was nothing more than a speck of dust in the shooting star that is New York City.

The *No Walk* sign shot red, but Oliver hadn't noticed, and the mongoloid grin on his face marched right into the back of Leo, nearly knocking him into oncoming traffic. Leo turned red and thrust his elbow into Oliver's lower ribs. That concluded the fantasy.

Five blocks south, they reached a place without a dusty, neon-lit sign. The doorman, early in the second half of his twenties, waited outside. He had a burgundy tie, cap, and jacket, and looked like he had been goofy enough to pour lead into people before he got clean. He gave the three businessmen a brief look and a briefer nod, then held open the door. No doorman in the history of doormen had ever been unhappier to let people through.

The city club was lavishly decorated with the usual Waspy requirements. All five floors were immaculately polished. One floor was a lordly library, two were eateries, and the others held granite steam spas, private conference rooms, and a few hotel suites for guests of the members. The only rules of the club were that all men must wear a necktie, and that phone usage was reserved for buttoned booths. Moses signed them all in and they climbed a staircase of slick wood and oriental rugs to the grill.

They sat in a cherry-leather booth and put their backs against the padding, so they could see anyone who came in or out. Heavy-hitting capitalists and Prada-wearing wives lined the room. Despite this sort of idealized society, it didn't seem like a fit for their mentor. When Oliver and Leo asked about his membership, Moses noted that it was an unrivaled source of business. The restrictedness of the club offered a sense of status, encouraging powerful players to apply. "Buy a meal here, and you've done two things—provided the most primitive of all human needs, and purchased someone's time. Remember what I told you though—it is equally important that you invite some to your table because they are deserving, and to invite others because they may come to deserve it."

Through their long tenure understudying Moses, the two cubs never heard anything like what he said next. "Oliver. Leo. You are the sons I never had. You took a leap of faith with me years ago, and I do believe that leap has been as rewarding for you as it has for me. I hope you understand that I must let you go out of admiration and respect. This may seem harsh, but it is reasoned. I want you to look at me, think of what I've accomplished and listen to my words. I do not want either of you to aspire for my life . . . to wish to be a guarded general of boardrooms. You are not me. And I don't want you to be."

Oliver and Leo gazed around the room of white-whiskered titans; how worn all their faces were. Moses then requested on'y one menu. Oliver and Leo were to go.

He closed their employment with, "All the accolades I've received, all the power I've taken, all the fortune I've built, none are the miracle I hankered for as a child. Business, as grand as it can be, can also be self-defeating. It can separate us as humans, and distract us from more purposeful missions. Remember that, as you return to the hunt. Farewell, cubs."

Those final two words hit Oliver like a brick: "Farewell, cubs." Oliver looked into his mentor's eyes and for the first time realized that the man before him was not an almighty colossus, but a boy.

Oliver then soaked up a truth that everyone learns at some point in life—every adult, everyone further along in life, is just an innocent little child at heart. Everyone is born into this world and forced to grow up, but we never lose that small kid within us. We hide behind our jobs and our egos and our social statuses and walk through life as best we can, but life eventually beats us down.

Oliver looked at Moses and saw how time had bludgeoned away at his mentor. And Oliver felt an immeasurable sadness ripple across his heart. He wished life weren't so tough, that we could learn all the answers. He just wanted everyone to be happy. *Is that so much to ask?*

Oliver stood, gored by this awareness, and accepted the reality that he had to leave everything he knew—again. The hour of bereavement arrived as the young men slid along the padded booth and took a long walk back to the street. It wasn't easy, but they managed to hold their leonine heads and imperial noses up as they left. They walked for miles as life sank in.

Gifted teachers are toughest on their most promising students. Moses had made them financially independent and blossoming prospects; he had seen their potential, and had helped them begin to realize it. But, when they thought more, did they really want to be his understudy forever? It was strange medicine, but they began to feel a new sense of freedom.

As they traversed the sidewalk, Oliver was deep in thought with a smile. *A good mentor in life is everything.*

THE HERMIT

THE CITY WAS an infernal, icy machine of flashing light—a pulsing skyline, a fortress. Somewhere in Tribeca, Moses and his wife would be finishing their sushi at their dining room table on the seventy-fourth floor. The spread would be world class. The rice would be so rich and delicate that it would explode like little clouds in their mouth. The steamed monkfish, the blackened seaweed, and the sashimi snapper would be superb. They would eat and overlook the convergence of the Hudson and East rivers into the Upper Bay, and the sun would be setting over Ellis Island by the time they laid down their chopsticks. Moses and his wife would open a bottle of something French, something *le meilleur,* and each savor six ounces by the fire before slipping off their garments to massage off the day in their whirlpool bathtub. Their favorite spa setting would take twelve minutes, then they would slide in bed and discuss the latest with their two daughters, one in her second year at UCLA, and the other in her third year at Princeton. Both were expecting three As, an A-, and a B+ to finish the semester. It would be 11:00 PM by now, and they would peacefully drift asleep.

Three hours later and three miles north, Oliver and Leo exited a dive. A week had passed since Moses turned them loose, and time was already eroding their gratitude. As a new suit grows old, loses its sharp color, becomes creased, the hems frayed, so too had their lives in New York.

With lubricated stomachs and uneven steps, Oliver and Leo entered the Library Bar, a respectable venue for respectable people.

The maître 'd, a girl of twenty-two or so, welcomed them. She escorted Oliver and Leo into the two-story room with bookcases for walls and leather chesterfield chairs. The busybody bit her lip and gave the young men an extra glance before retreating in her black dress. Her game was precise and practiced. The bar was her roulette wheel and she was the marble.

The bar was near empty, but they decided to continue poisoning themselves with a fourth order of vodka. They crossed their ankles with a yawn, and gaped around the room, antennas up. Curiously, a hermit had nestled himself in the corner with a book open in his hands. He was still and quiet, and looked sober, and this horrified the young men.

The thing about people who fully abstain from alcohol is that they are either the only sane breed on our planet, or they are secretly more sinister than the rest of us. Either way, Oliver and Leo needed to know.

With the hermit's slender nose deep in a text, Leo called out to him. "What can be so interesting at this hour?"

The hermit looked at them like a man who had better things to do. "This little book here is my own. It is my central instruction on life. Many of its words were written long ago, but their truths endure time."

Now this was different. Oliver inquired, "If that book's really yours, why continue to read it? Why not seek more advanced material?"

The hermit was a frail man weighing 145 with feminine arms and a gentle face. "I once thought that way, that I must seek more. Then I came to realize that all advancement derives from the fundamental."

Homer moved over and shook hands with the young men. Then

he took a seat. "Our world is a sea of convolution, so it can be helpful to review the basics before I tread into complexity. Some days you will sail along calm shores, others will catch you in a storm. But, if you have a set of principles to guide you, placid and choppy waters are equally navigable."

"Okay . . . I buy it. But how did you figure out all these endurable truths?"

"By taking my time. By committing to continual self-improvement. By listening to life as it reveals itself."

Oliver pointed to the journal. "May I?"

Homer pulled back a bit and patted the spine. "I must insist. Let life teach you. Craft your own principles from your own experiences. You are young. Pay attention and you will learn exactly what life needs you to know."

Deterred, the young men placed another order for vodka. Seeing discouragement, Homer reconsidered. "Perhaps I can share one." Reopening his journal, he searched long enough for the round to arrive. "Here we go." He extended his slender finger onto the page. "People will come and go in life. Some will teach you how to become a better version of yourself, and others will teach you the opposite. Learn the difference and you will steer your sail in the right direction. Then develop the courage to set out on your own path, even when it means losing people along the way. As you learn to say no to things that don't matter, you will begin to say yes to things that do."

Oliver and Leo applauded with smirks across their mouths. Homer was offended. He rose and loudly cleared his throat. "Maybe one day this will sink in, perhaps when you aren't murdering your minds. Look around this room. Thousands of years of wisdom sit before you. Spend a little time alone now and then. Invest in yourself and figure out what you're after. Self-improvement is a noble pursuit, and what you are doing tonight is not."

Homer then exited.

It was now 4:00 AM and the young men were plastered to the

hairline. The wily maître 'd snuck over and notified them that they needed to close out. When their cards cleared, she pushed them to the coat check, and just inside the door. Leo put his arm around the busybody and placed his hand a bit too low down her back. He spread his fingers, kneading her thin black cloth and trying to figure out the mechanics of her dress. In the height of modesty, he thanked her for her attentiveness.

The maître 'd debated playing his game, knowing that if she succumbed they'd neck around for a bit, then give each other the time. But as Leo spoke, she caught the dreadful stench of his breath, and began to think of all the obscene places his mouth had been. And instead of drinking in his words, she began to regurgitate them onto his collarbone. She hit eject and stored Leo for reference.

The bundled young men receded through revolving doors and out to the wintry climate. The night air cut. No cabs came. They considered the subway momentarily; only, when they looked down the cold stairwell, that notion froze. At this hour, if they descended beyond the turnstile guarding the rail, they would arrive in an excessively dirty dungeon with shabby people who were closer to death than to eating breakfast. If the young men could outwait the impending robbery, twenty-five minutes would go by before they would hear the agonized squeal of a metal skeleton grinding to a stop. There was zero chance they were walking down those sadistic steps, so they about-faced and moved towards home in the desolate air.

They walked and they walked, twenty blocks down to their apartment in the scrapyard of the night. This was not your chipper skip-along-with-intermingled-arms, twirl-around-lampposts kind of walk. This was brutal. This was dodge-the-consonance-of-falling-icicles and hope to hell that you have ten fingers and ten toes by the time you reach your door.

They traveled south with their liquid blankets into SoHo. Five years before, they had taken a tiny but insanely expensive, flex-two-bedroom apartment on the fifth floor of a walk-up in the East Village. That blank unit had cracked floors, a kitchen smaller than a bed, and a bathroom smaller than the kitchen. They had adequate salaries when they started, but after federal, state, and municipal taxes, their rent consumed 45 percent of their after-tax income.

Now, though, they had ascended to a previously unthinkable level of compensation, and spent at a previously unthinkable level too. They upgraded to a three-bed, three-and-a-half bath loft in a building with a security guard and an elevator that opened in their living room.

Half an hour later, as they crossed Houston Street, there was an air of familiarity in the moment for Oliver. He was just unsure whether he was remembering something he had done, or something he had to do. Moving along, Oliver caught something faint but unmistakable lurking in the periphery of his vision. What he saw hit like Novocain—the luminescent butterfly fluttered across the pavement beside him.

He halted midstride, his face frozen like a block of ice. Any degree of wildlife was unlikely in this concrete morass, but this . . . this was unworldly—a hot blue comet in the stiff black night. Oliver watched the glowing wraith float as the shadows twisted around its wings.

The sapphire butterfly danced over to a billboard rolled down the back of a building. The mural was of a revealing model in red-petal lingerie. She was a golden girl with a full face, deep-blue eyes, soft brown locks, and a smile meant for the heavens. A woman who pulled a million a head for any eligible suitor who came her way. The photo was her standing in front of palm trees, surfers, and sunshine. She was standing in California.

The butterfly hovered on her perfect nose and sat. Oliver cast a line through his mind, trying to reel out any association for what he was seeing. The butterfly sat patiently, waiting for Oliver to infer its message.

In the chilled air, a gust of warmth brushed Oliver's cheek and settled deep in his chest. In this moment was happiness. Oliver thought back to his and Isabella's first night together on the beach. How distant that now was. Oliver stared at the phantom until a guiding sense clicked.

Something fey was once again speaking to him. And once again, Oliver listened.

THE LITTLE GIRL

THE VELOCITY OF life again accelerated, and the great oracular disk of time expanded beyond reach. Five more years passed after Oliver and Leo moved west in their own Manifest Destiny. Memories of their days wayfaring across Europe were primly limited, as they were now, assuredly, men. Men who could not escape their learned habit of success; men who were caged by their own occupational savviness. Or perhaps it is more accurate to say that these men never sought to escape their cage. Perhaps, they couldn't see their own tether. Their new business endeavor took them outside of real estate, but not outside of investing. The idea took months to blossom, and when it had, it came in an unlikely location.

Oliver was strolling through a shopping center when it came. He watched as hundreds of people harvested visible rewards: new purses, new outfits, new shoes—all tangible items labeled in advertising as must-haves. Oliver watched these people, and realized how alienated he felt from society. He felt isolated from a culture that bought into the illusion of stability, from a crowd dependent on a false system.

As Oliver strolled, he lightened as he looked back on his hardships and all that he had learned. He thought back to his time with the clothier. He thought about how he had grown happy when life was simple.

Oliver knew he needed to surround himself with people he and Leo were philosophically aligned with. He knew he needed to meet other driven individuals who were willing to handle the discomfort of leaving the herd, people who were innovative and intellectually curious, those who asked the right questions and went after what they believed in.

Later, Oliver imparted this idea to Leo, who asked, "What if we went a step further, and invested in them?"

And, with that question, what began as bold entrepreneurial confidence, as a courageous bluff, flourished. Their venture capital firm turned into a unicorn of an operation, and their portfolio skyrocketed in value. Not only were Oliver and Leo able to multiply their assets, but they were able to select the monopolistic startups which did so, and help run them. Their business had erupted. It created thousands of jobs and attracted top talent from across the world, and the City of Angels increased its economic output with their success.

But despite fiscal prosperity, Oliver was far from wealthy. He had fallen under the spell Mr. vom Glas warned him about. Oliver's life was full of cash, but void of love, and he grew irritable. He made himself civil, and met many women, but when he'd take them out he would quickly grow discontent and disconnected.

This was the nest Oliver built for himself—high and dry. He bordered on narcissism. He was apathetic outside and discontent within. No longer did he ask who he was supposed to be. He just rode the tides of life, and never bothered to look back.

The small, fuzzy lemon jettisoned upward, eclipsing the sun momentarily as Oliver summoned the torque for his thunderous serve.

Oliver spanked the chartreuse sea-urchin across the tennis court, where Leo returned it with a backhand and pushed his friend into a tense volley. The rally played out in lethal ballet of nimbleness and cutting ball placement, and spectators around the country club were awed as the assassins chopped the ball back and forth.

At match point, all their training was a backdrop as instincts took over: a whistling kick serve from the backline, a topspin into the crosscourt, and a displaced drop shot from a net charge. Oliver was the victor but feared what waited for him off the court.

Cheryl was a beauty with rolling locks of black hair. By miracle, she'd roped roped Oliver into a date last week. He sheathed his racket and set a towel around his neck, rushing to leave as quickly as he came, hoping to avoid the conversation.

"Oliver! Oh, Oliver! Come here a minute, will you, doll?"

The chirp came from a table in the shade. Oliver stepped over with an indifferent face as Cheryl looked down at herself. "See anything you like, dear?"

She was smiling in her sundress, looking great. Oliver stiffened. He examined her outfit and hair style. Her eyes shone with desire and optimism as he cracked his neck and spun out of the conversation, parading away while chanting the urgency of showering and other dull excuses.

When he reached his car, Oliver tossed his bag in and plugged the ignition. Hundreds of horses roared with the turn. This was morphine to him. His pearl white Ferrari F40 throttled in place. Onlookers drooled.

Oliver rolled out of the club as his mind began to wonder. He pitied the many who saw him in his car as some sort of prestigious individual, some sort of archetype of a person who they might look up to. He thought of the lonely bartender, the overworked schoolteacher, the stressed executive, the eager intern, the underpaid fireman, and then himself. He wondered if anyone was happy. Oliver then felt a magnificent burden heave onto his shoulders—something he never thought possible. Atlas took the world and thrust its weight onto Oliver's back, and Oliver crouched over, with a knee beneath Olympus, wishing that everyone could see him, in a dream car, in a dream home, without a dream in his heart. He just wished that everyone could realize how unfulfilling life is without love.

Heading home, Oliver's stomach reminded him that he had yet to eat. He wheeled into the parking lot of an organic grocer. When the receipt was in his bag, Oliver was walking towards the escalator leading out when a mother and her three children cut him off. Initially, he was distraught at the inconvenience of being stuck behind this slow-moving caravan, but something so unlikely and so simple interrupted his grievance.

The two young boys stepped onto the escalator first, followed by the mother with the shopping cart, and the little girl, about four, was last.

Oliver inched forward to the moving stairwell when he heard a whimper. "Mommy!"

The little girl was frozen with fear at the edge of the landing, scared that she might be sucked into the motor or get her toes clipped. The mother hadn't yet noticed, and the girl began to sob.

Oliver's heart disintegrated.

He shifted his groceries, knelt, and offered his hand. She took it so quickly, so harmlessly, so ignorant to anything beyond the idea that this stranger would help her, and they stepped on and descended together. The little girl stopped crying, but her eyes were teary when she looked up to Oliver and thanked him. It was the most sincere, genuine, caring thank you he had ever received. When they reached the lower landing, her mother was looking up at the scene. She thanked Oliver, and everyone went on their way.

Oliver reached his car and flipped up his driver door with a smile. Children are the brightest souls in the world, and he had provided her a sense of security in her moment of vulnerability. This little girl, this source of light, reminded Oliver that there was still an ounce of love left in his bulletproof, metallic chest.

Oliver lived on the Pacific coast. While he and Leo had built a supertanker of a company, he lived in a modest home for the size of his trust. The white-shuttered, deep-blue bungalow nuzzled against a paved stretch of waterfront. Despite its charm, the house was merely a place he lived—not a place he belonged. Oliver had been looking to belong for a long time.

Downstairs in his bachelor pad, he stood over a drink cart and tossed two ice cubes into a glass, gripped a bottle and effused a double over rocks. Oliver mixed drinks with a heavy hand, preferring to coat his synapses well if he was bothering to do so at all. He ascended to the roof and a tropical dusk. He sipped slowly, pausing to luxuriate in the comforting burn of the liquor, then lay down in a hammock and slung his mind out over the ocean. Soon, he dozed, and in the dissident chambers of his mind, surrogate thoughts dripped in.

Oliver rustled awake before dawn. He looked out over the ocean at the sun peeling over the horizon and saw something even brighter float by.

Just off his roof, the butterfly waltzed in the wind. The ethereal spilled over as he thought he heard the eidolon speak to him. The butterfly had a recognizable voice . . . an infinite, dominant voice. It said, "In darker days, there lived a man who once thought as you do."

People say things get worse before they get better. But this was too much. The sapphire butterfly was a cloudy chimaera running amok in Oliver's mind. Elements from his time with the horologist were now developing corresponding coordinates in his brain.

Oliver had long ago chalked up the butterfly as a mental imprint, an illusion, an insane hallucination, but now he found himself calmly reassessing that idea. The flat circle of time was inverting in a spiraling inertia of lucidity, because he now knew . . . the butterfly was real.

Oliver watched it hover. He watched its simplicity and the arduousness it endured fluttering along the coast. He listened as it spoke again.

"Often a man is labeled as cold when he is only sad. Oliver, your chest is a frozen cavity because you still miss the one person who made you feel warm. You must again find your path. Do not stay as you are, in misery and remorse."

He thought of Isabella. He thought of her with him, her dimpled smile staring into his caring eyes. The butterfly drifted away like a hang glider above the triangular ocean spray. He warmed in the bliss. Isabella was back on his mind.

THE STUNNER

"CAN YOU IMAGINE if we'd stayed home?"

Oliver and Leo were reminiscing on Ocean Avenue. The scene was transitioning from a casual setting to a throbbing nightclub when she walked by, and her pretenses were not unnoticed.

She had hard Slavic lines to her face. She was exotic; objectively beautiful with a hint of danger. Leo watched her from their chaise. This stunning woman paraded around the lantern-lit patio looking like a mondaine. She didn't notice Leo until she crossed in front of his table, but when she did, she wanted him to get a good look. At the bar, she turned around to face the crowd purposely and lithely. Her brazenness and audacity were alluring.

When she made her way back, Leo wiped his chin, rose like a panther, and excused himself from the conversation.

An interval passed as Oliver sat alone at their table. When the bill was paid for, he scanned the scene once more but still didn't see his friend. Finally, their server explained that he had seen Leo on the way out with some "stunner" of a woman. Oliver supposed that this meant two things: that Leo and this woman had hit it off, and that she didn't have any friends with similar looks.

But that was that, whether Oliver liked it or not. He chuckled at the inanity in how men act around women. *Every man for himself,* he guessed.

A bassinet of seasons brushed by, and Leo and Alessandra were engaged. It had been a year and a half since they met, and it was clearly going to work out.

Tonight was their engagement dinner. The venue was chosen for its revered views and known to be a setup nearly impossible to secure, but Oliver had an "in" with the chef. The dinner guests were impressed at Oliver's prowess; the move was a massive, plutocratic flex, and no one doubted it would be a momentous occasion.

Champagne buckets lined the table along with prime cuts of meat and agreeable sides. The banquet was well along when Oliver, unfashionably late, entered to applause. He half waved, half self-destructed as he edged towards his seat wearing the plastic smile you show when you're trying not to scream. As he moved around the table toward his seat, he noticed it was cluttered with top-shelf drinks ordered on top of his bill.

All the guests seemed to have the glossy, droopy eyes of being drunk, but some had that extra layer of pupil dilation; at these debutante gatherings, half the attendees pregame with a variety of octagonal and circular pills proven to minimize paranoia in 98 percent of test patients. Take one or two with alcohol and it becomes a narcotic cocktail that overloads your dopaminergic pathway like the hollow thumping of riot guns in the street. The thing about drugs is: the bigger the town, and the richer the crowd, the stronger the sedative.

Oliver reached his chair. He greeted his and Leo's parents—who had flown over for the celebration—and then Alessandra and her family as well. Again, Oliver eyed the length of the forty-top table to estimate the bill. These guests, these spendthrifts that he hardly knew and definitely didn't like, were racking up a king's ransom on his card. His card! The one with no spending limit. He must inform the sommelier or the hostess or the busboy to cut everyone off before his credit card went nuclear.

But when the cocktail waitress came to him, he said nothing. He shook his head politely, flashed that plastic smile, and placed an order for a martini.

Throughout the night, guests rose from the long table and came over to thank Oliver for hosting. They strained to say things that would arouse him, but he only scowled and tilted his martini and let the stuff burn his throat.

The dinner progressed with Oliver deflecting transparent flattery. His only genuine responses were to his parents and Leo's, while with everyone else he spoke in evasive measures meant to crush the commenter. With all the attention homed on Oliver, Alessandra, the stunner, the fiancée, particularly buxom on this night, let out a little gasp and gazed out to the restaurant as if she were renouncing her guests. She kept shooting Oliver furious looks, clasping the glass in her hand, threatening to reduce it to shards, needling and prickling him as if he were intentionally stealing the spotlight from her. Oliver had yet to figure out the facial expression that would let her know he was equally unpleased with the attention, so he redirected the focus by clinking a butter knife to his glass. Oliver stood and straightened his tie before speaking. "I'd like to thank you all for coming here tonight. I've known Leonardo like a brother, and now Alessandra like a sister."

He continued for a few minutes, then got stuck when he began to speak of the meaning of love. With blank, dry eyes, Oliver ended it with the look of someone who wanted to say more, but didn't. Alessandra's small, blood-red lips receded to a thin sliver across her face, and Oliver could sense the line of tension that would always be between them.

The night concluded with Oliver, in a dignified state, staring out a window over nocturnal Santa Monica. Everyone was tipsy and laughing and enjoying themselves, but he turned his back on the guests to let them sizzle.

Oliver leaned against the glass, and looked out into the world. He stood in a gulf of solitude, thinking onerously about the roads he hadn't taken, the options that never were. He looked back at his loving parents and Leo and Alessandra, and everyone close to him, and winced. He returned his gaze to his reflection in the glass, and asked himself, "Who have I become?"

Oliver then looked out beyond the window. The street below was full of whistling cars and cheerful people. Oliver envied them. It didn't matter who. *Them.* He envied the depth of their pleasures.

If you are intelligent or cynical, and especially if you are both, most of life is the same, and it takes a miracle just to feel alive. Oliver had felt anesthetized for a long time. He had reached the pinnacle of success, but for what? He didn't feel like anything was better. His soul had been on a sharp decline since Isabella. He thought of her, in bed with him, ankles crossed, lounging in lace covered only by his T-shirt. Her smile.

Oliver thought about how fake he'd become. His world was a game, a façade, and while he sometimes drew pleasure from it, he could feel real life flowing by. He had helped so many people throughout his illustrious come up, and now it was time to help himself. Again, Oliver found himself at a crossroad; he had to choose between that which he had become so accustomed to and something he had wanted a long time ago. A deeper existence.

Oliver congratulated the couple, wished his parents goodnight, and pardoned himself home. When he arrived on his seafront boulevard, his heart was like a cloudy, cerulean oyster. He needed to reopen it and find the pearl. He needed to relearn how to love himself.

It was the day after the newlyweds returned from their honeymoon. Oliver invited Leo for coffee on this balmy morning.

The moguls were casual today as they rode electric bicycles along the beach. Their favorite coffee shop was between buzzy and deserted when they arrived, and conversation quickly became philosophical.

"Think of the coffee bean, Leo. It is a product of life. The soil nourishes the plant. The plant produces the bean. The bean becomes coffee, and the coffee runs through me and flowers into an idea. It's all a big circle, isn't it?"

Leo returned a long, wet slurp. His face had a look that said, "This is all very nice, Oliver, but what of it?"

Oliver's tone turned serious. "I have to tell you something, Leo." He cleared his throat. "At the end of the week, I'm resigning from our company. You're fully capable of managing it yourself, and I couldn't ask for a better partner in business, or for a better friend. I hope you're up for it, but I know I'm leaving things in good hands."

Leo nearly bit his cup. He began to set his coffee down, but at the last moment he reversed and took another sip. Leo choked on this one, so Oliver detailed his proposal of resignation. By the time the bottom of their cups revealed ceramic, they reached an agreement.

"When the market hears about this, things might get shaky. You'll have raiders and secondaries lined outside the office trying to buy our portfolio. Be professional. Be agreeable. But don't waver. They'll say it's all business, and that they're relieving you from a headache, but business is always personal, and don't let anyone ever tell you different."

Leo questioned what was driving the decision. Oliver truthfully responded. Buried behind his tone was absoluteness. He was telling his oldest friend something he had never told anyone, something to be said in confidence, then never repeated.

"Years of secret suffering have taught me self-control, Leo. There have been so may days when I've asked myself, *Where this is all going?*" He stopped and looked out into the day. "You know, when I was younger, I thought I'd figure out my purpose in life when I knew what

I wanted to be when I grew up. Then we went off on an adventure and I thought I'd discover it out there. Then I thought it'd come when we took the job with Moses . . . then when we started our company . . . but the answer hasn't arrived. I've kept convincing myself that what I'm looking for is just over the horizon or around the corner, but it's not; it's within. There's been a steady undercurrent of change in my life, and when I saw you and Alessandra and our families so happy, I realized that I was not. I've been quiet since then. I backed away from my convictions just so I could remember that kid who wanted to be a hero in this life . . . who wanted to inspire people and make the world a better place. I had to step back to see that I've grown numb and forgotten who I am."

"It's her, Oliver, isn't it? You've never really let her go. I've never seen you look as happy as you did back then."

Oliver's eyes fell to the table.

Leo spoke. "You know, I used to be jealous of you. I think that's why I really left Barcelona—I envied what you had. Even after we met back up, I admired your pain, because at least you'd felt the sting of love. And now that I have, I can't imagine life without it. I want you to be happy Oliver, so go and try to get that sting back, even if it means reopening a painful wound."

"It's taken me so long to figure out who I am, Leo."

"Only because you have such a good understanding of who you are not, Oliver. And that is invaluable."

Oliver smiled like he had when they were young. "I feel like I've just been running away from the past, and it's finally caught up with me on this side of the world. After I left Isabella, I thought the change in environment would help. But that's been my recurring mistake: to hit eject. Now look at me. My path led me to this dreamland of a life, yet I find myself so upset. It's like running away is exactly what doomed love depends on."

Oliver leaned back in his chair and pointed to the ocean. "You can be in the most picturesque place, but if you don't have love within, you can't love the world around you. It's not about where you are or what you're doing; it's about who you're with when you're in those places doing those things."

The chair of the board sat before a three-course breakfast in Beverley Hills. She was by herself, but not alone. Outside, her assistant was verifying the day's schedule in a black sedan idling in place. On the chairwoman's head sat a short patch of off-white hair. She had a giraffe neck and a pear-shaped body, and looked remarkably polished. Against explicit instruction, her breakfast was interrupted when her assistant rushed in to notify her that Oliver had tendered his resignation only ten minutes before. The rest of the board was calling for a meeting that night. The chairwoman accepted the adjustment to her calendar.

The board meeting was swift and nonnegotiable. Oliver was firm with his decision and suppressed most of the questioning. The chairwoman expected this, knowing Oliver for his reputation of taciturnity and secretiveness. She spoke for the board as they navigated through the situation. The chairwoman was professional and understanding, and she reluctantly accepted his tender on one condition—that he see the company doctor to assess mental stability.

When Oliver heard this arbitrary term, his eyes widened. "Fine."

Eager to rid himself of the nuisance, Oliver stopped in the doctor's office the next morning. He expected it to be no more than a formality, but the doctor was far from passive, far from the pediatrician who spouts off thick, honeyed layers of babble to patients. This doctor behaved like a military sergeant with an inferiority complex. Oliver guessed that he either had an outstanding lawsuit for malpractice, or, more likely, that his third wife was cheating on him—though it was strange for him to be so infected with emotion when he was so displaced from love. The thing about marriage is that for ten people out of a hundred it's a fairy tale. For forty, they work at it. And for the rest, it's not practical. So people get divorced, and the first breakup really is tough. But after that, it's more about economics than romance; it becomes transactional, a habit. So, why was the doctor so mad?

Oliver sat on the crunchy white covering of the examination table. The paper cover was supposed to sterilize the room, but really it was a ruse, probably left there for weeks at a time, only serving to comfort the patient that this doctor wasn't the kind you might hope a wounded Nazi got. As the interrogation progressed, it became clear that this tenured physician completely relied on a few patented drugs whose manufacturers had swiped him up off the record. So not only was this character unethical, but he had no understanding of the mechanics of the system in play.

Oliver was shameless for the whole appointment, answering laundry questions like "State your name," which isn't even a question, with "Don't you know that?" The physician said he did in a low, throaty growl.

There was a series of these interactions, leaving the doctor frowning in consternation. Then the open-ended questions came, giving Oliver more room to trifle with his surveyor. He had the doc glued to his stool as Oliver intentionally put forth naïve questions and was rewarded with amusing textbook recitals. The sport was excellent against a nonplussed mind, and quickly it revealed the doctor's ignorance in nutritional science and primitive psychology. Oliver squeaked by with a passing grade, pretending to wipe the sweat off his brow. "I'm sane. Thank you, Doc."

He stood in the corner of the office, scanning the skyline out the windows. If he turned directly around, across monochromatic carpet was a heavy walnut door. To his right was an Ateliers Pinton rug made of a wire, bamboo, and wool, and on top were four cubical, cream-white leather Le Corbusier armchairs with stainless-steel frames. And set perfectly in the center of all this was a glass coffee table with a dark-green hardcopy of *The Atlas of the World* by Oxford University.

To the left of this conversation area was the workspace. The L-shaped desk was perpendicular and crisp at each angle, half of it raised over the other so that paperwork could be stored from sight but remain in reach. Three sleeping computer terminals were anchored to the surface next to a stainless-steel phone and a slender lamp. The chair behind the desk and the shelving behind the chair were part of the same set. And on the clean walls were black-and-white originals from known artists.

Not a soul had been in the office when Oliver's secretary showed the mayor inside—a portly, sweeping man around five-seven with a forty-six-inch chest. He wore a double-breasted brown suit with a boring blue tie and a boring blue shirt. His cheeks were puffed like he was constantly holding his breath and his chunky lips reached ear-to-ear below his undersized nose. He examined Oliver's office with a degree of rivalry, and impatiently tapped on the dial of his watch. He was the mayor! He had the upper hand here. Everyone bowed to his political power. Why was he in this office, alone, waiting?

The phone exploded for the seventh time. The mayor leaned against the armrest of one of the cubical chairs, crinkling the leather, as Oliver came in looking like a million bucks. He was smiling and wearing a checked grey sport coat, tailored, navy chinos—no pleats—and a white dress shirt, dark circular sunglasses, brown loafers—no tassels—and no tie.

Oliver had no idea the mayor was visiting until his secretary told him in the foyer. Apparently, the national press had picked up the story about Oliver's departure and splattered it across front pages and TV screens.

When Oliver entered, the phone was singing away. He greeted the mayor and leapt towards his desk, but when he reached over and lifted the phone there was only the sound of the dial. Oliver set the phone outside its bed and let the buzz lag inside the earpiece. No more calls.

He took a seat across from the mayor and eyed the deterioration of his leather chair. The mayor's posture straightened as he spoke with a fluty voice.

"I heard the news, Oliver. I must say, you retiring so young brings a bleak outlook to our economy. I've had council members and lobbyists and business owners calling me since dawn, and you know what they've all said?"

Oliver was dying to know what this carrier pigeon of corporate interests had to say.

"They say you've gone over the wall, Oliver. That you're crazy." The mayor said this like it was most precious nugget of information he'd ever given out for free. He let out a small chortle. "I've assured them you are not. But I'm curious myself. Why now?"

This was exactly the reason Oliver wanted out. He wanted to not owe anyone an explanation, to lounge wherever he saw fit, and to unglue himself from his desk and be left alone to pursue something deeper than money. Inside, Oliver laughed at his own foolishness. Being an executive was far from the glamorous first-class fflights and Michelin-star dinners broadcast in the media. It was more about overbooked calendars and boring conferences with people you barely know. How wrong he had been.

"Oliver?" The mayor bent his neck down, expecting an answer.

Oliver addressed the staple topic without mentioning the emotional baggage that he had confessed to Leo. He outlined his philanthropic interests, and focused his speech on the accession of an authentic Henri Rousseau painting he would endow to the Museum of Art.

The mayor hung on his every word as if this idea were the most brilliant thing since sliced bread. Oliver thanked the mayor for all that he had done, and left him blushing as he escorted him to the elevator.

Back in his office, Oliver placed the phone in its cradle but quickly decided to unplug the line altogether. Rumors had spread about potential takeovers, and everyone wanted in on the action. He then went back to the white chairs near the blue rug and clear coffee table, trying to figure out what he'd do next in life. Oliver found his mind rigid and inflexible. His head flooded with strategies for new investments and considerations of economic trends, as he was unable to detach himself from the career he had worked so hard to build.

Oliver slid forward and opened the hardback atlas on the table. When he opened the cover, on the first page in sapphire letters was a note that had never been there before.

Oliver leaned back, crossed his legs, and placed the book across his lap. The note read:

> *As a young boy, I was anxious to grow up. So, I imagined myself as a man. I imagined I would be strong, and full, and happy.*
>
> *I have now become a man, and I realize that I am none of those things. But I do know why. To be strong, I must allow myself to be weak. To be full, I must allow myself to be empty. To be happy, I must allow myself to be reborn. So, to truly be who I am, I must give everything up that I am not. And that, I can still do.*

THE SUPERCENTENARIAN

OLIVER WOKE FROM a black well of sleep to find himself sitting in his living room. Last night, he lit a fire and fell asleep watching it burn. He was surprised to find the fireplace still crackling. One little ember on top of the ash had refused to go out. Oliver sat and watched it glow. The little ember showed no signs of wavering. It still had the roar of a fresh fire in it, and in a final stand, it sparked up like a Molotov cocktail. The little ember thundered and flexed and burst into a micro explosion over the ash. Oliver didn't flinch as it swelled up into a little mushroom cloud in his living room.

This had no effect on Oliver as he tightened his core and stood to shower off the night before. He returned, exfoliated and composed, and made his way into the kitchen. He checked the time. He was behind schedule. Oliver spooned espresso grounds into his presser, and while the machine began its crunching, he opened the fridge. With full arms, Oliver moved towards the blender across the way, but there was some kind of a pull at his feet. Each step away from the little ember became more and more weighted, and finally, the force pulled him onto the floor and his supplies scattered across the tile.

Oliver turned. He couldn't see what was pulling him. Slowly, he was dragged across the room until he was right in front of the pit.

The ashes began to foam.

Locked to the ground, Oliver could only watch as the ashes foamed into salty spume, bubbling, waiting to be unleashed. A wave of water suddenly curled up from the ash before pouring over Oliver. The severe celerity knocked him into a churning undertow as the surging water flooded his home. Oliver was thrashed about in the current and swept out into an unknown, amorphous sea . . . and he lost consciousness.

Salt water splashed his face as a gentle tide frothed up and down. He turned over to find himself along the sand of a tombolo. To his left was a small hill covered in tropical plants. To his right was a larger island, lush with forest and dense with peaks. Directly before him was a long strip of sand connecting the rocks on his left to the isle on his right.

He stood. The ocean at his feet was a crystal green. He looked into the horizon, where rippling whitecaps crossed over a reef. This was the most idyllic stretch of paradise he had ever seen. Nothing else was in sight.

Then, like the little ember, something exploded in his chest. His knees buckled as he fell back to the tide, feeling like he weighed nothing at all—like the shell of the man Oliver had become had blown away.

He stood again, renewed. And over his shoulder, the sapphire butterfly appeared. It was different this time. The butterfly floated before Oliver with patience. It wanted him to follow. He tailed the apparition across the tombolo and up the rocks. They climbed the hill up to the peak, and sitting on the crowning ridge top was a home. The home was simple and high-minded, and wonderfully vibrant and cooperative with its surroundings. Around the structure was a glistening garden and glowing and open sky.

On the crest of the property was a woman. She was mending and aerating a flowerbed, and the air around her was full of dancing gold specks. She looked full and total, like a woman connected to the loveliness and depth of existence.

When she noticed Oliver, she smiled him over and lent her finger to the butterfly.

"Hello, Oliver. I am the supercentenarian." The white-haired woman was in fine shape, with smooth muscles and bright skin. Her eyes were a pale greenish glitter, like a forest pond tucked away in the trees, with a single beam of light piercing the canopy. Wearing a sunhat and gardening garb, she directed Oliver to a patch of roses with the same sapphire and pink stripes as the butterfly.

The supercentenarian spoke in ubiquitous terms. "Such a beautiful thing—life." She bent over the flora and caressed a petal. "You wouldn't guess, but these flowers were an accident. They developed a strange condition early on but somehow grew into these lovely things. Tremendous beauty can arise from the flawed, don't you think?"

She then lent the butterfly finger to Oliver. The gentle creature lifted, fluttered, and landed in his palm, but when it touched down in his hand, it passed away as a haze of blue-and-pink smoke wafted into the heavens.

Oliver gasped at the lifeless shell in his palm, then looked at the supercentenarian like some poison within him had brought death. "I'm so sorry, I—"

The supercentenarian spoke softly. "Don't worry, Oliver. The butterfly has always been this way."

Oliver looked at her with questions in his eyes. The supercentenarian addressed him with a didactic tone. "Sooner or later, we all go back to where we came from. Yes, the path we all take to get there is our own, but sooner or later, we all go back."

She folded Oliver's fingers over his palm, cupping the faded wings in his fist, then wrapped her hand around his and placed it over his chest. "The things around you do not affect your heart, Oliver. It is your heart that affects the things around you."

She turned from the garden and climbed the redwood steps inside. Her home was a single large room with the same degree of flora and life as outside. Brilliant slashes of white sunlight filtered in through green masses of vegetation and hanging gardens. The floor was part pebble seed and part zoysia grass, and a river ran through the middle with a soft waterfall at one end and a deep pool at the other.

A pair of cushions sat on the lawn next to the river. The supercentenarian offered Oliver a seat and handed him an empty tea cup. She returned with boiling water, bent over, and laid the butterfly inside the cup, slowly steaming the perfume from its wings.

The supercentenarian nodded him on.

As Oliver sipped, the tea dissolved in his mouth in a gasified osmosis, like he was absorbing light. A radiance began to fuse within him—something limitless, something he had felt before, like his heart had healed.

The supercentenarian took a cushion beside the stream. "You have been listening to the butterfly for some time."

"Yes, but only when I could not look away, when it caught me off guard. For years, the butterfly frightened me, as I thought I might be going mad. Now, I find myself saddened by its passing. Something tells me I have failed the butterfly, that I have missed its meaning."

"The butterfly has much to teach us, Oliver. It is a creature of frivolity. But even with all its beauty, the butterfly is only a suggestion. It chose to show itself to you when it wanted you to think, when it wanted you to look inside yourself and decide which path you might take. Oliver, life is an endless crossroad, in which we are presented different options each day. Once, you knew your path, and you walked down it with faith. Down that road was happiness, fulfillment, and purpose. But somewhere along the way you changed your direction, and it was you who chose to do so. The butterfly has simply been a guide to get you back on track."

Oliver took in the tea, listening more.

"You have been so anxious to improve your surroundings, yet so unwilling to improve yourself as person. Your readiness to run has prevented miracles from happening in your life, and you have paid dearly for it. What you now seek eludes your sense of sight, and is therefore invisible. It eludes your sense of hearing, and is therefore soundless. It eludes your sense of touch, and is therefore bodiless. Kings and queens have spent fortunes trying to find it, but they always come away empty handed. Do you know why, Oliver?"

He shook his head.

"Because, they did not let go. To find what you are looking for, you must shed the idea of who you think you are and who you think you should be. Become vulnerable and empty, and what you are looking for will find you."

The supercentenarian then asked Oliver to assist her in the garden. They drifted back out to the calm day and trimmed and watered and cultivated the patches. When the work was complete, they reentered her home. Together, they took their places beside the soft waterfall once more, drank the sapphire tea, and sat in silence—Oliver was to wait.

Minute by minute, hour by hour, day by day, time passed in this peaceful cycle of gardening and meditation and tea drinking and fasting. And once again, life was simple. The heaviness of who Oliver once was began to recede, and a fresh coat of regeneration began to accumulate over his heart.

THE HOROLOGIST

ONE MORNING, THE supercentenarian spoke to Oliver. "If you go into the garden, and decide to go deeper and deeper, instead you will emerge at the gate."

Oliver exited her home and strolled outside. He was on the backside of the house when he reached down to pluck a sapphire rose from the mulch, and like a lever, when he uprooted the flower, a plume of a smoke rose into the air and a young butterfly soared out of the ground.

Oliver lent his finger, but the butterfly hurriedly encircled the house. It fluttered and fluttered, and when Oliver came around front, instead of the garden there was an astral gate. The cosmic sieve did not lead up or down, left or right. The butterfly fluttered in with a hither here, a thither there, and thrice more.

Oliver followed, and he became so captivated by the butterfly that he lost track of where he was, and with a single flash of hard white light—a blink, a photovoltaic shock—the butterfly was gone.

Oliver turned in a circle. There was nothing but whiteness in every direction. He walked forward in the white abyss, blind and uncomfortable and utterly vulnerable, but he kept moving. There was no direction in this place—no dimension.

He kept on until a black door appeared before him. He flipped the parallelogram knob, but it wouldn't open. He could feel its loose frame, like it had been fitted in ancient history, so Oliver gripped the handle with a simultaneous flip and lift and pushed with all his might. This time it opened.

He entered a narrow hallway with black-and-white checkered tile and a black runner rug resting on top. At the end of the hall was what looked like an identical door to the one he had just entered, and on the wall to the right were vignettes of Oliver, lined up in black frames.

He examined the first one. The vignette made him look abstract and geometrical. He shuffled along the rug studying each portrait of himself. They were arranged in reverse chronological order. The farther he moved, the lighter the color of the frame and the more realistic his features grew. In fact, the last one was photographically exact. It was Oliver, as a boy, in a fine white finish.

He reached the second door. It was a polished, flush sister to the one through which he had entered. This one opened with ease. It was new.

The Bel Étage was mute and pressurized. Oliver had never noticed how vast the restaurant was. The ivory dining room was astonishing, with thirty-foot drapes the color of snow, lined with gold trimming. The mammoth glass wall stared into a white horizon, the same photovoltaic purgatory he had come from. But now in the distance were hints of black lightning, like a deadened channel of cybernetic web.

All the tables in the dining room were empty except for one. Seated across the Bel Étage, Oliver saw *himself* as a boy wearing that same seven-fold tie and virile suit. It was the boy from the final picture frame, a living construal of his inner-narrative. Oliver's face fell apart. It wasn't that he had gone backward in time—it was more that the flat circle of time had defibrillated and convulsed into a single, dense core.

On the near side of the table was an empty chair. Oliver walked across the dining room but didn't sit. Suddenly, the words he had once heard came back to him. Oliver looked at his younger self and thought, *You act like you have it all figured out . . . but you know it as well as I: you are much more than you pretend to be.*

The boy then spoke to Oliver. His younger self had the eyes of a possessed ghost. "Some days, when I rise, I have memories of tomorrow." Each letter came out like a bullet.

Oliver removed his fingertips from the back of the empty chair and sat. The silent constellation of empty tables in the dining room weighed on him as Oliver looked across the table and stared at who he was once. Then he spoke softly in a crystalline voice. "For some time, I have wondered how you can be so awake, yet so unaware of your potential. So, here we are . . . and in more ways than one, it is the examination of your destiny which brings us together."

But the boy didn't respond. There was a conception between Oliver and the boy; his words bounced off a two-way mirror, like a shadow melting across glass. Oliver was about to reach his hand across, wanting so desperately to speak to his younger self, to tell him what his life would be, to warn him, when he heard, "Sir, for dessert . . . we have the rarest selection. It's from old alchemy, from something eternal. Enjoy." Oliver turned to find the horologist holding a small plate. On top was a small white ingot encaged by a black mesh of epitaxial growth. It reminded Oliver of another era.

Oliver looked from the plate to the horologist. There was something in those deep eyes now that he couldn't read. The horologist set the selection on the table, halfway between Oliver and the boy. He then reached into his jacket and pulled out the alloy clock and set it beside the plate.

The horologist spoke across modulated static. "Did you know, my friend, that if you were to live a hundred years that only amounts to 876,000 hours? I've never heard anyone say that before. 876,000. That's not very long. Why do people live as if they have all the time in the world, when life is hardly a wisp in the wind?" The horologist's voice was heavier than it had been. "Whether people accept it or not, Oliver, the day they are born, their hourglass is flipped and the sand begins to fall." He rolled the case of the clock on the cloth. "Tick. Tock. Tick. Tock."

Oliver grabbed the horologist by his sleeve. "What is this?"

"I think, Oliver, you know."

"A choice?"

"Yes, a choice of the preternatural—a final solitaire, if you will. There is only one piece of time available in the alloy. Either you or the boy may have it."

In the horologist's eyes were the ancient beginning and the eternal ending of the universe. He spoke with wisdom not based on knowledge or experience, but on something innate.

"I am in a very important line of work, my friend. It surpasses all rational understanding, but this was the only way I could design it. At any one moment, the world is at once being pushed out of, and pulled into, existence. Time is an endless balance of life and death."

The horologist looked down at the alloy. "This clock, the one I made for you, is unique. It is the first of its kind. Oliver, this clock can be reset, but it comes at a cost."

"What happens to the boy?"

"I can't be sure. Time, and its abiogenesis, does not enjoy being anticipated. But I'd like to think he will grow up to be a nice little story. We can't quite know though, can we? Like I said, this is the first of its kind."

The horologist took the pocket watch and opened the face, glossing his thumb over the dial. There was a sense of satisfaction there.

"What we can know is whether his story will have a chance. You now sit at the supreme crossroad, Oliver. I am offering you time, something I've never been able to do."

Oliver stared at the boy for a long moment then turned to the horologist. "Time is three-fold; it is three fortunes at once. There is what we say, what we mean, and what we do. What we say is forgotten. What we mean is lost. But what we do is all we really have. For my whole life, I have tried to get a grip on time. I grasped at it, but it always slipped through my fingers. Maybe I've never gotten my hands on it because it isn't there in the first place. So here I sit, thinking of who I've become, and I know that if I let go of what I am, I may grow into the person I was meant to be. And all I now have, all that I've ever had, is a choice. And I intend to make the right one."

Oliver felt a sense of purpose and cosmic identity. He ever so carefully lifted the framed skin of the selection, set it in his mouth, and crushed it with his molars.

The next moment engulfed itself in a supernova. And out of the chaos, out of the sapphire flame, came a little creature. There was a flutter here, a flutter there, and thrice more.

EPILOGUE

OLIVER LOOKED AT his reflection like he recognized himself for the first time. For a few moments, he sat in motionless wonder as he looked at his image in the water. He was a boy again. He stared deep into the lake, and somewhere beneath, somewhere not here nor there, he saw a blur of something sapphire and radiant and ubiquitous behind him.

He turned, but all he saw under the moonlight were the dark foothills near Isabella's home.

Oliver stood. He could sense a fresh, beating heart in his chest. He greeted the world with a smile that had long been forgotten as he walked beneath the stars, up the hedged lawn and into the pink-caper garden to meet Isabella. It was the night he left.

When he saw her, he once again fell into the slipstream of love.

And they were on their way.

AUTHOR'S NOTE

WRITING HAS A stigma, which I must address.

Society tends to believe that novelists design complicated plots, then proceed to fill in the holes. The real process of authorship is much less structured. Stories arrive foggy and obscure. They come as characters whispering in your ear, characters who are a part of you, and it is your job to give them life.

So, if you have an itch to write, please don't think of authorship like you're standing at the base of Everest. Just take time each day to allow your story to bleed out. The plot, the timeline, the dialogue, will come as they will. Just write, and remember that if you have a story inside of you, the world deserves to hear it.

Of course, writing is not for everyone, but I strongly believe that each person has a medium for their artistic expression. It may be painting, or singing, or acting; but whatever it is, develop it and use it as a tool to learn more about who you are. Life's answers come from within; you will not find them anywhere else.

So, why did I write? It's simple. I wrote because I had to. I wrote because I took great pleasure in developing the characters, the story, and the timeless messages planted throughout this novel. Nothing more. Nothing less. I just loved the process. Find what you can wake up on a Saturday morning and do for fun, then fall in love with the idea that you might become successful doing just that.

I had remarkable help and guidance crafting *The Horologist,* so I must take a moment to thank a few people who have been so kind as I've defenselessly exposed myself in this book.

A particular acknowledgment must be extended to a few people: Joan Hester, Michelle Manos, Cindy McCabe, Susan Smith, and Polly Caprio,, thank you for editing this text, and for providing tremendous wisdom when it came time to deepen the impact of my words. Lisa Maher, thank you for taking time to shepherd me on the publishing path, and for providing guidance on the jejune lapses which flowed through my draft manuscripts. I am indebted to you both.

To the Koehler Publishing team: wow. Thank you for believing in me and for taking a chance on an unknown young man. You all caught so many mistakes and unnecessary scenes in even my most-polished manuscripts.

To my friends: I needn't thank you. That is why we are friends. You prop me up when I am down, and I know that I have strong bonds to lean against. Our ties will only grow stronger.

You may be wondering if I'm going to acknowledge my colleagues. Here's the thing: I don't believe in that word. You should work with people you like, people you can count on, and people you enjoy spending time with. So, if you're reading this and don't like your job, find a new career, or develop your own source of income. Just don't keep doing what you're doing. It's not worth it. Time is too precious.

Of course, where would I be without my family? You have been there to deal with me from the beginning, and I've not been easy. And I will be there with you to the end. No words can capture my appreciation, but I'm excited to show it.

Lastly, to the Isabellas of the world. Find the man who will do anything for you, and don't settle for anything else. That is the deepest lesson that I've learned in all this. It is okay to love, and it is okay to fail, but it isn't okay to not try at all. If every person in this world keeps their heart open and their spirit strong, our planet will be better for it.

It has been a great pleasure.

Consider me a friend,

MILES

CPSIA information can be obtained
at www.ICGtesting.com
Printed in the USA
LVOW10s0921210518
577925LV00002B/126/P

9 781633 935983